KAROS

Star-Crossed Alien Mail Order Brides

SUSAN HAYES

ABOUT THE BOOK

Looking for love on all the wrong planets? Try the Star-Crossed Dating Agency.

Karos might have survived the war on Romak, but it left scars on his body—and his heart.

Now he's on Earth, assigned to guard the first alien embassy. His purpose is simple – protect his new home and everyone in it. This time, he won't fail.

This book contains a bodyguard who can kick ass in high heels, and a war-weary dragon who is about to learn that love is the only battle you have to surrender to win.

SUSAN HAYES

Karos (Book #7 of the Star-crossed Alien Mail Order Brides Series)

First Pring book Publication: September 2019

Cover Design: crocodesigns.com

Editor: Dayna Hart

Published by: Black Scroll Publications

ISBN: 978-1-988446-52-3

ACKNOWLEDGMENTS

I want to thank my friend Ruby for answering my questions about First Nations programs in the military, and for supplying me with Girl Guide Cookies without judgement.

CHAPTER ONE

KAROS HAD to give the humans credit – they were persistent. From his vantage point on the top floor of the joint Pyrosian-Romaki embassy, he had a clear view of the bedraggled group of protestors gathered outside the gate. Their signs were sagging in the driving rain, and the winter wind was colder than a snow dragon in a snit, but they kept coming back. Day after day, they stood outside and chanted their hate-filled slogans.

They were swaddled in so many layers of clothing they were barely recognizable, but he could name each and every one of them. They were the faces of the Humanity First movement, the ones too angry or too stupid to hide their identities. They weren't the real threat, though. The danger came from the ones whose names they still didn't know, the ones who had taken over after their leader, Justin Kines, had been captured months ago. He and his lieutenants were in custody, but they refused to cooperate, or even speak to anyone since their arrests.

Justin had been convicted of orchestrating the bombing

at BC Place stadium more than a year ago that had killed dozens of Pyrosians and put a strain on the newly-forged bonds between the humans and the rest of the Inter-Planetary Council.

The Council had previously agreed to allow humanity probationary status, but some of their members were concerned that humans, as a species, were too young and volatile to be allowed access to the collective knowledge and technology they were being given. Blowing up a sports stadium hadn't done anything to quell those concerns. The daily protests weren't helping, either. While most of humanity had welcomed the Pyrosian and Romaki, there were still those who let their fear of change consume them. The fear and doubt on both sides were a continuous source of concern for everyone involved.

Karos had witnessed this same cycle of fear and distrust on his planet when the rulers and the temples had gone to war over the future of the Romaki people. After a year of fighting, the worst was over. The power-mad priests were defeated, the ruling families had prevailed, and the healing had started. Not for him, though. As a member of the Royal Guard, he'd been in the thick of the fighting. He'd done his duty, defending the king of the Fire Dragon Clan and reclaiming the future for all Romaki, but the victory had come at a cost. His soul was soaked in the blood of too many beings whose only mistake was giving into their fear.

He had tried to move on, but his homeland was haunted, and so was he. When he heard about the embassies on Earth, he'd volunteered immediately. It was what he needed --a fresh start, and a clear mission: protect the embassy, and show the humans there's nothing to fear. He could do that.

The door behind him opened. "I thought I'd find you up here. Do all dragons like to brood from the heights, or is it just you?" Jet asked in English. It was standard practice to speak the local language during work hours, even though the humans employed at the embassy had been given cognitive enhancements that allowed them to speak both Romaki and Pyrosian.

Karos pointed to the protesters. "I'm not brooding. I'm watching."

"Pretty sure you were doing both." The dark-haired Pyrosian diplomat joined him outside, though he was careful to stay beneath the overhang that sheltered them from the wind and rain.

Karos snorted and glanced over at Jet. "If I were brooding, you'd know it. I'd be on the roof, glowering down at that lot in my dragon-form."

Jet grinned. "If you ever decide to do that, let me know. I want to be there when they look up."

"It won't be any time soon. Too damned cold and wet. Does it ever stop raining in this city?"

"According to the locals, not for two more seasons. If you're going to spend so much time up here, you should probably invest in some wet-weather gear."

"No need." Karos idly flicked out the fingers of his right hand and muttered a brief incantation. There was a shimmer as the magic took form, and the patter of raindrops changed to a low, sizzling hiss as the water hit the barrier he'd summoned and evaporated.

"Nifty trick."

"If you ever find a female who can put up with you,

you'll be able to do something similar. While our magic comes from different sources, there are similarities. I've been teaching Keth and his mate new ways to manipulate his flames."

Jet nodded. "Keth mentioned you'd shown them a few things. He's hopeful that Radek can start teaching the mated Pyrosians back home the same skills. It will be a few generations before our military is back to their former strength. Until then, any advantage is welcome."

Karos chuckled. "I see you're in full diplomat mode. No reaction at all to my jibe about females."

"I have my life exactly the way I want it. I have an entire planet to explore, a job that I actually enjoy, and the better part of a galaxy between myself and my parents." Jet grinned as he said the last part.

"There is no distance great enough to stop a parent from trying to interfere in their children's lives if they want to."

Jet snorted. "So I've learned. Still, it's an improvement. Since I'm on Earth, my mother thinks I have a better chance of finding my mate than if I were waiting for her back on Pyros."

"The amount you socialize with the humans, she's got a point. You talk with them all day, and almost every night you head off to dine and dance with them. If your mate is in this city, she must be a recluse."

Jet clapped him on his shoulder. "As a diplomat, being social is part of my job. I'm improving human-alien relations."

"If it's your job, why do you insist on taking me with you? I'm in charge of security, not socializing."

"Two reasons. One, because you need more fun in your

life, my broody friend. And two – one of these days I might cross paths with some of them." He inclined his head to the crowd below. "When that day comes, I'd prefer to have a magic-wielding dragon at my side."

"I've seen you training with the guards. You can protect yourself well enough." He'd been surprised to discover the Pyrosian nobleman had kept up his hand-to-hand skills since his stint in the military.

Jet shrugged a shoulder and grinned. "I might be a diplomat, but I'm also a realist. Words don't always work, and unlike my mated brethren, I can't summon fire with a snap of my fingers. Punching is the next best defence. Still, if it ever comes to a fight, I'd rather have you around. You are what the humans call a serious badass."

He appreciated the compliment, but he'd learned quickly that it was best not to encourage Jet. About anything. Ever. "Save the flattery for the humans. They seem to appreciate it."

Jet scrubbed a hand over his jaw. I'm not sure even my highest compliments are going to work on our next visitors."

Karos nodded. He'd heard rumours about today's guest. Hanna Dewan was a very determined female with extensive wealth and influence. She was also dedicated to a singular cause: rescuing unfortunate human females from their abusers. Sex slaves, war brides, victims of cultures who refused to value female life. She had saved countless females, and she was coming here to discuss a bold venture – rescuing more of these unfortunates and sending them to Pyros, where females were treasured because of their rarity.

"I don't think flattery will work on a female who

spends her life fighting for the rights of those who have none. The direct approach might be best."

"Likely. I've already arranged for the princess and her friends to join the meeting remotely. Short of bringing Ms. Dewan to Pyros to see for herself, that's the best I can do."

"Would she be willing to make the journey?"

Jet chuckled. "Not everyone is as averse to long voyages as you. I should be leaving soon. I'm meeting Ms. Dewan and her party at the airport."

"Do you need me to come along as security?" He didn't enjoy these meetings the way Jet did, but protecting the embassy, it's staff, and all visitors was his duty.

Jet shook his head. "I'd rather have you here, keeping an eye on them. I need to show Ms. Dewan that we can provide a safe, comfortable life to the females she is trying to protect. If those fearmongers start anything while she's here, it might give her reason to doubt."

"I'll see to it they remain quiet." If he had to, he'd transform and go for a short flight. That always seemed to subdue their protests for a while.

"Thank you."

"If I'm staying here, who will go with you?"

"Kyle is driving, and I thought I'd take Vykor with me."

Karos smiled. Vykor was a good choice. He had a calm, quiet manner the humans seemed to like, especially the females. The young dragon had been almost overwhelmed by all the attention he's received since his arrival. Back on their homeplanet, Vykor was a pariah, but here? Here, he was a celebrity, albeit a reluctant one. "Good. He's been hiding too much lately."

"Says the male standing alone on a rooftop in the rain," Jet drawled.

"I have been told I make some of the humans on staff nervous."

"I think it's the growling."

Karos had to stop himself from doing exactly that as he glowered at Jet. "I don't growl… much."

Jet laughed and turned to go. "We'll work on your social skills another time, my friend. I'll see you later."

After Jet left, Karos pulled a small, flexible tablet from his back pocket. He activated it with a touch, swiping through various live security feeds until he found the side gate used mainly for deliveries. It was quiet, and the alley running past it was empty. If there were any problems, he'd send word to Kyle to return using that gate instead of the main one. He set the tablet down on the railing so he could easily see the screen even while watching the protestors below.

He was responsible for the safety of every being within these walls. They trusted him to protect them, and it was his honour to do so.

I won't fail them. He vowed to himself as he stood watch, his hands gripping the railing so tightly it dented. He hadn't been there the day his friends had needed him. The day they'd died. He wouldn't let that happen again.

MEGAN LET the conversation flow around her as they made their way across the tarmac, huddled beneath the umbrellas their hosts had brought with them. They'd been met at the steps of Hanna's private jet, both men – males, she corrected herself – dressed in dark, perfectly tailored suits. The males looked to be in their mid-thirties, but since neither of them was human, she couldn't be sure. The dark-haired one was Jet Tindor, the Pyrosian ambassador. He'd introduced the young blond with him as Vykor of Romak, though she noticed he didn't mention the male's clan. *Interesting.* From what she'd read, clan affiliation was important to the Romaki.

Curious, she glanced at Vykor's eyes. She knew that fire dragons had gold eyes, while snow dragons had silver ones. Vykor had one of each. She had no idea what that meant. There wasn't enough information available yet, which was why they were here. They needed more information about the Pyrosians, their planet, their culture, and anything else they could learn.

Everything looked good on paper, but Hanna wanted to be certain before she committed to anything. That diligence was one of the many things Megan admired about her boss. Hanna was a rare breed, a woman of means who had devoted her life, and her wealth, to helping others. Guarding her wasn't just Megan's job, it gave her a chance to be part of something meaningful – the Haven Network.

She let herself fall a few steps behind as they approached the limo, sweeping the parking lot for potential threats. Hanna's mission put her at odds with warmongers, mobsters, and sex traffickers all over the globe, and more than one of them had tried to have her killed. Megan's job was to make sure that didn't happen.

Once they were all seated inside the luxurious vehicle, Megan sat back and watched the interplay between the humans and aliens. Vykor and Jet sat on either side of her boss. Hanna and the Pyrosian were speaking intently, and she could tell by Hanna's keen expression that she liked what she was hearing. Jet was animated but intent, and she got the sense he was truly listening to what Hanna had to say.

She turned her attention to the other member of her party. "How you doing, Lily?"

Hanna's personal assistant offered her a weak smile, but her cheeks were pale, and there was a greenish tint to her skin that matched her green eyes. "I'm fine."

"Trained investigator, remember, I know when you're lying." Megan reached into her pocket and pulled out a couple of ginger chew candies. "Here. These should help."

Lily gave her a grateful smile. "Thanks. I was fine until we hit that patch of turbulence over the strait."

"Yeah, I got queasy, too. It took a couple of those candies and a lot of deep breaths to get my stomach to behave."

"I didn't know the T-800 models could get airsick." Lily unwrapped one of the chews and popped it into her mouth, her eyes glinting with laughter.

"Which is yet more proof that I am not a terminator model. I'm a flesh and blood human, just like you."

Lily shifted the candy to her cheek. "Humans sleep. They also tend to fall down and bleed when someone shoots them."

"If I'd gone down, we wouldn't be here. It's part of my contract--no bleeding until the danger passes." Lily had been teasing her about being a cyborg since they'd been attacked on the way to a safehouse in Asia. Their attackers had been angry but disorganized, and Megan had managed to hold them off until help arrived. A bullet had grazed her arm, and another had ricocheted and got her in the calf. It hurt like hell, but neither injury had stopped her from doing her job. That was what she got paid for, and Hanna was a generous employer.

"And sleeping? When was the last time you got eight hours sleep?" Lily asked.

She shrugged and glanced past the younger woman to the rain-soaked world outside. "I'll sleep when I'm dead. Until then, I have too much to do."

Lily peeled another ginger candy and settled back into her seat, her attention moving back to the conversation between the Pyrosian and Hanna. Lily was as dedicated to her job as Megan was to hers. Lily was Hanna's right hand, making things happen and ensuring their boss had everything she needed to get things done. They'd worked together for several years now, and Megan considered both Hanna and Lily family.

She kept one eye on the traffic that flowed past the windows as she reflected on how long it had been since she'd been home. Well, home wasn't really Vancouver, but it was close enough to make her think of family. She hadn't told her parents she was coming, in case there wasn't enough time to squeeze in a visit to the lands of the Tsawwassen First Nation, where her family lived. She didn't want to get their hopes up.

Hope. That's what this trip was all about. The Pyrosian race was at risk of extinction. They had come to Earth in hopes of finding genetically compatible females to help rebuild their species, and discovered they were not only compatible, but that humans had interbred with Pyrosians before.

At first, they'd come in secret, but now, there was open

trade with not only the Pyrosians but also other members of the Interplanetary Council. Humanity suddenly had access to technology and knowledge that would have taken centuries to acquire on their own. The world was a more hopeful place as the new information was slowly disseminated, bringing mankind into an age of enlightenment. At least, that was the goal. For now, there were still too many places shattered by war, where people were ruled by violence and fear. The Haven Network was a means of escape for the women and children trapped in those places, but once they escaped, they needed someplace to go. Somewhere safe. That's where the Pyrosians came in.

Hanna hoped that the distant planet could become a place of refuge for these women and their children, even if they weren't matched to a male as a potential mate. The rulers of Pyros were open to the idea, but working out the details would take time, and possibly a trip across the galaxy so they could see for themselves where the women would be living. When Megan had taken Hanna's job offer, she'd known it would involve a great deal of travel, but she never dreamed it might involve leaving the planet.

That was a long-term problem, though. Her immediate concern was the Humanity First activists. Despite the arrest of most of their leadership, they were still a threat. Some of them were protestors for hire, others were anarchists who would move on to the next cause, but there were still too many true believers, and those were the most dangerous of all. She'd been part of the RCMP's protective policing services at one time, responsible for safeguarding diplomats and world leaders while they were on Canadian soil. During her time there, she'd learned all about the threats posed by terrorists, cartels, lone wolves, and the mentally unstable.

The Humanity First movement was very active in Vancouver, which wasn't surprising given that this was the place the Pyrosians had made first contact. It was also the location of the aliens' largest embassy and the site of the first attack. The bombing of B.C. Place stadium had been intended to drive the Pyrosians away, but instead, the aliens had only increased their attempts to educate and befriend humanity. Still, everyone associated with the aliens was a potential target. If anyone learned what Hanna was doing here, it would increase the threat level. As far as Megan was concerned, the longer they could keep Hanna's presence here a secret, the better.

She sat up and did another casual scan of the traffic outside. The rain was heavier now, making it difficult to see much. They were heading away from the city center, which meant the traffic was slowly thinning as they made their way to the embassy.

The need for secrecy meant they had flown into a private airfield and were relying on the Pyrosians for transport and hospitality for the duration of their stay. Leaving security decisions to others wasn't the way Megan preferred to do things, but it had been necessary this time. She still didn't like it.

Hanna caught her eye and gave her a small smile, so subtle it wasn't likely anyone even noticed. She flashed one of their hand signs to her at the same time, a quick lift and lower of her index finger that meant "all is well."

Megan raised her hand to respond, but a shadow caught her attention, and she turned her head to see a massive dark shape hurtling toward them.

"Hold on!" Her shout was all the warning she managed before the other vehicle slammed into them, the impact sending the limo into a violent spin that threw them all against their seatbelts. Her ears were assaulted by shocked cries, the screech of tearing steel, and the squeal of tires as they careened across the rain-slicked pavement.

Her senses still spun even after the car came to a stop, and she had to swallow hard several times to quell her nausea. "Everyone okay?" she asked as soon as it was safe to open her mouth.

Everyone muttered a shaky affirmative. Score one for safety testing--they were all in one piece. She checked the windows but couldn't see anything but the empty road. Where the hell was the other vehicle?

"Lily, call 911. Mr. Tindor, can you contact the embassy?"

The dark-haired alien nodded and pushed back his sleeve, revealing a communicator strapped to his wrist. "Immediately."

"Thank you." She undid her seatbelt. "I think we were rammed intentionally. I'm going outside to take a look. Everyone else stays here, and lock the door after I'm gone. Vykor, if anything happens, can you transform and get the others out of here?"

Before Vykor could answer, the partition between the passenger area and the front of the vehicle opened a few inches.

"Kyle, you okay up there?" Jet called to the driver.

Megan turned her head toward the partition and asked, "Did the other vehicle drive off?"

Instead of replying, the driver pushed something

through the gap, and it fell to the seat beside her. The partition closed again. *What the hell?*

She blindly grabbed the object Kyle had dropped, her other hand already trying to unlock the door. It wouldn't open. The thing in her hand started to hiss, a stream of something cold flowing over her fingers.

"Everyone, cover your mouth and nose. Try not to talk or breathe fast," she ordered before covering her mouth with the sleeve of her jacket. Even as she did it, she knew it wouldn't be enough to stop the gas from affecting her.

Everyone frantically tried their doors as the gas continued to flow, filling the interior of the limo. *Shit. Shit. Shit.*

She spun in her seat, muttered a soft "sorry," to Lily as her head landed in blonde's lap, raised both legs to her chest and kicked at the window with her high-heeled shoes. If they lived through this, she was going to give Hanna hell for insisting she change into business attire before they left the jet.

The impact jarred her from toes to teeth, but the window didn't budge. She pulled her legs back and kicked again, pouring every bit of strength she had into the blow. This time, the window starred a little around the impact point of one heel. Her head was swimming, and her legs were getting heavier by the second. Her third kick hardly made it to the glass at all, and she didn't have the strength for another attempt.

Lily's body went limp beneath her, and she looked up to see the blonde slumped against her seatbelt, eyes closed, jaw slack.

It took all the strength she had left to turn her head to check on Hanna. She was unconscious already, and both

Vykor and Jet were fading fast. Reality hit, bitter and cruel. She'd failed. They were going to be taken, and she hadn't stopped it. Neither had the aliens, and one of them was a damned dragon.

That's the last time I trust the aliens.

CHAPTER TWO

KAROS WATCHED THE PROTESTORS INTENTLY. Something had riled them up about ten minutes ago, and the sudden change in activity had him concerned enough he had sent word to Kyle the driver to divert course to the side gate on their return journey.

The protesters had charged the gates *en masse*, yelling their slogans and waving their signs in a coordinated frenzy of activity. The embassy's guards had taken up position inside the gate, their expressions impassive, but even from where he stood, Karos could sense their tension.

When his communicator buzzed with a priority tone, he answered it without looking down.

"Karos here."

There was no response.

He glanced down at his wrist and touched the device again. "This is Karos. What is it?"

Still nothing but dead air. A chill ribbon of dread wound around his spine as he checked to see who had tried to contact him. When Jet's name appeared on the screen, the sense of dread grew stronger and erupted into full-blown fear when his device erupted in a strident series of chirps. Jet had activated his panic alarm.

"Frost and fire!" He touched the screen of the tablet, calling up a tracking program with hurried swipes of his fingers. Where were they?

The program located the limo and displayed it as a red dot on the screen. It was only a few blocks away, and it wasn't moving. Worse, the vehicle's tracker was the only one showing. There was nothing from either Jet or Vykor's devices.

He dropped the tablet into a pocket. "Call security, front desk." He almost growled the command. There was a soft chime and the sound of an outgoing connection. The second someone answered, he started barking orders.

"Send a security team to Ambassador Tindor's location. Clear all gates, and notify law enforcement to meet me at the scene." He paused, then added. "And have them arrest the protestors out front. They're accessories."

"Yes, sir. And uh, accessories to what, sir?" the Pyrosian on the other end asked.

"I don't know yet. But it's nothing good." He switched off the device, put it in his pocket, and banished the barrier spell with a wave of his hand. The rain pelted down on him, soaking him within seconds. He ignored it and set a hand on the rail.

"*We go?*" His dragon asked, already pushing against the confines of his mind.

"*Yes.*" He vaulted over the railing and summoned his dragon. The transformation happened in the time between heartbeats. One moment he was falling, the next he was soaring on powerful wings. He climbed hard and fast, a roar tearing from his throat as he headed toward the last coordinates he had for the limo.

Flames and fury, if something had happened to his friends, he'd show those Humanity First fools exactly why they should fear their alien visitors. He'd burn them all and scatter their ashes to the winds.

His mind raced as he flew, trying to fit the pieces together. The protestors normally did nothing but stand outside, brandish their signs, and chant. Today's sudden surge of activity had to be connected to whatever had happened to Jet, Vykor, and the humans. The timing was too suspicious.

It didn't take long to reach the vehicle. He tucked his wings and dropped into a dive, streaking out of the sky with a full-throated bellow that should have sent any humans diving for cover. Nothing moved.

He extended his senses, looking for hidden dangers, and found none. Everything was quiet. The limo was damaged, the entire back half crumpled on the driver's side. It had been knocked off the road, streaks of rubber showing its trajectory. It hadn't moved since coming to a stop and sat abandoned on a weed-choked boulevard outside an empty lot.

He landed without bothering to shift forms, his massive body taking up most of the street as he furled his wings and lowered his head to look inside the car. The air was thick with some kind of noxious odour that stung his nose, making it impossible to smell anything else.

The interior was dark, and it took him a moment to see the figure sprawled across the seat, her dark dress blending with the shadows. He growled, and the figure moved slightly, her efforts sluggish.

His dragon stirred within his mind, suddenly agitated about something, and he snapped his head up, expecting trouble. There was nothing but the soft patter of the rain on the hood of the vehicle.

"What is it?"

"Ours?" The beast responded, the thought accompanied by a sense of confusion and general agitation.

"You're not making sense." He didn't have time for riddles right now. Jet and the others were missing, and the only one with any answers was inside that vehicle.

"Smell something. Want."

That, he did understand. He wanted to talk to whoever was still in the vehicle, too. He shifted forms, conjured a dry set of clothes, and stomped over to the door.

"You. Inside. Come out slowly, hands first."

There was a soft, feminine groan from inside the vehicle, and his dragon reacted with a shout. *"Want. Take. Ours!"*

He ignored the creature and focused on the only lead he had in the disappearance of his friends. Sirens began to wail in the distance, and he knew he only had a few minutes before human authorities arrived. He needed answers, and he needed them now, before the humans came with their rules and protocols.

"What happened?" the female asked.

"That is what I want to find out. Come out here, hands first."'

"Where's Hanna? Lily? And who the hell are you?" The female demanded, her voice still groggy but gaining strength with each word she uttered.

He gritted his teeth. "I do not know where the others

are, which is why I need to talk to you. Get out here. Now."

The female didn't answer, but he heard her moving inside.

"We are running out of time. Your authorities will be here soon."

"My authorities? You're from the embassy, then." She finally moved into view, and he assessed her quickly. She was tall for a human female, with a powerful frame hidden beneath her clothes. She had sleek, jaw-length dark hair, burnished gold skin, and eyes the colour of the forests that covered the mountains outside the city, an interesting blend of greens and browns.

"I am. And now you're going to tell me what happened, and why they took everyone else but left you behind."

Her eyes narrowed as she left the limo, her movements carefully done to allow her to extricate herself while limited by the knee-length skirt she wore. "They left me behind because they knew I'd be nothing but trouble." She took an unsteady step toward him and the heel of one impractically designed shoe gave way, sending her tumbling toward him.

He acted on instinct, catching her and pulling her to him to steady her, and as he did, his dragon roared in triumph. *"Ours!"*

Her scent wrapped around his senses and understanding hit like a comet. The female was his *sadina* - his mate. Only she could not be. She was human. And he wasn't worthy of a female. *"Teska ren,"* he muttered. This couldn't be.

This was why I hate wearing heels.

The new arrival stepped in and caught her before she could regain her balance, hauling her up against his big body with almost effortless strength. It was like being cradled against a warm brick wall. The man was *huge.*

His dark red hair hung almost to his shoulders and was highlighted with streaks of silver, mostly at his temples. He stood at least six feet tall, and beneath the almost military cut of his dark clothes was a whole lot of muscle. He was staring at her with golden eyes, his jaw set in a hard line that did nothing to detract from his good looks. He looked like he'd walked off the set of an action movie, and he was most definitely cast as the hero. She looked up at him and reassessed her estimate of his height. She was five-foot-nine, and he was a good six inches taller than her. He was also staring at her as if she'd grown a second head.

"Uh, thanks for the assist." She straightened and tried to move away, but his arm was locked across her back and she couldn't move more than an inch in any direction.

"Mind letting go of me, now?"

"Sorry." He said in English, letting go of her and stepping away so quickly she almost felt a breeze. He stared at her from a few feet away, his golden eyes unreadable. "I am Karos Zattar of the Fire Dragon Clan. Who are you?"

"My name is Megan Richards. I'm…" She swallowed as a wave of guilt struck. "I work for Hanna Dewan."

"And yet they left you here. Did you have something to do with the attack?"

"The only thing I had to do with the attack was being too slow to stop it from happening." She glowered at him, resenting the accusation he'd lobbed at her. "I'm Hanna's bodyguard. It's my job to protect her, and I failed. She and Lily are out there somewhere, and I need to find them, not stand here while you accuse me of being the bad guy."

"You are her bodyguard?"

She bristled. She'd been dealing with comments like his since her first day of training. "Yes, I am, and until today, I had a perfect record of client safety."

Karos sighed. "I meant no offence. Given your role, I'm surprised they didn't do more to incapacitate you."

"Honestly, so am I." She'd been unconscious. They could have killed her. Why hadn't they?

He gazed at her for a moment, then flashed her a fierce smile that bared his fangs for a second. "Would you like to make them regret their oversight?"

"Hell, yes." She kicked off her wrecked shoes and tried to ignore the squelch of cold, wet mud as her bare feet sank into the ground. "What about you?"

He folded his arms across his chest. "I am the head of security for the embassy. I will make them pay for this. If you wish to be included, you may join me.

He was the head of security? Then he had a lot to answer for. She gestured to the limo. "Today, I trusted you and your people to do *my* job, and now my friends are missing. Why should I trust you again?"

His golden eyes narrowed and a muscle in his jaw jumped, but instead of the argument she expected, he bowed his head and uttered a tired sigh. "My friends were taken, too," he reminded her. "We must have missed something."

Sirens were coming their way now, and judging by the way the sound was bouncing off the walls, they were approaching from several directions. They were almost out of time. "Considering it was your driver who gassed us? I'd say so, yeah."

"Kyle was part of this?"

"He's the one that tossed the gas canister into the back of the limo." She looked around, suddenly realizing the big man was alone. "How'd you get here so fast?"

"Ambassador Tindor activated an emergency beacon. I used the vehicle's – I believe you call it a GPS – to locate it."

She looked around. There wasn't so much as a bicycle to be seen. "But how did you *get* here?"

He jerked a thumb at his broad chest. "I told you, I am of the Fire Dragon Clan. I flew."

Right. Dragons were real. And they weren't from this planet. "Of course you did. Because you can do that."

He flashed her that primal smile again, and her pulse kicked up a couple of notches. Then, her mind was overtaken by a powerful impression of what it would feel like to feel those fangs of his grazing down the side of her neck as he moved over her, their bodies – whoa.

Where the hell had that thought come from?

He drew in a deep breath, his nostrils flaring as if he'd caught wind of something. Then he growled at her, his gold eyes burning with something that made her breath catch. She took a step back, then stopped herself. She didn't back down from anyone, not even growly space dragons that thought they were in charge.

The rumble of approaching engines was audible now. He glanced toward the loudest source of sirens, then back to her. "You need to make your choice. Work with me or with the police."

"You're not going to work with them?"

He gave an almost imperceptible shake of his head. "I will not obstruct them, but they are bound by rules that I am not. Which will it be, Megan Richards?"

"I still don't trust you." She said, weighing her decision.

"Understandable, but not relevant."

"Are you always this bossy?"

"Yes." His mouth softened in a hint of a smile. "At least, that's what others have told me."

"If we do this, we'd be partners. If I liked taking orders I'd still be in the R.C.M.P."

He chuckled. "The trick is to hold your temper long enough the ones in charge eventually promote you, so you become the one giving the orders."

"So I've heard." She held out her hand to him. "Partners, then?"

He crossed to her and took her hand in his much larger one, and she couldn't help but notice the callouses on his fingers and the firm confidence in his grip. "Partners."

Something else happened when they made contact, a rush of pure lust that made her sway toward him. She was attracted to him, but it wasn't like anything she'd ever felt before. It was so strong she had to fight the desire to touch him, to run her hands through his hair and explore the hard lines of his body. She dumped a mental bucket of ice water on her libido. She didn't know what was going on, but she had more important things to focus on right now. Like finding her friends and making sure the ones who took them learned the error of their ways.

He released her hand as the first police cruiser appeared, closely followed by several more cop cars and two dark sedans with tinted windows and diplomatic plates. She looked from them to Karos and gave him a brief nod. She was on team embassy, which meant that, like it or not, she'd follow his lead.

"Now we have that out of the way, I'm going to try tracking my friends." She ignored the incoming vehicles and went back to the limo to retrieve her purse from the floor. Relief hit her when she found her cell phone still tucked inside. She turned it on and activated an app she had hoped she'd never need to use.

"You can track them with that device?" He asked, coming over to stand beside her, his gaze on her phone.

"Maybe." People exited their vehicles and headed their way. In a few seconds the questions would start. She stared at her phone. The program synched, chimed, and opened a new screen. It was blank. Hope took a flying leap off the nearest cliff and landed in a shattered heap at the bottom. "Dammit."

Karos uttered a disappointed grunt. "Nothing?"

"No signal. Which means either the kidnappers disabled their phones and trackers, or they're so deep inside a building the signal can't be detected." She put the phone away but left the app running. If it got a signal, it would sound an alert. It was the best she could do. For now.

They both looked up as they were surrounded and hit with requests for identification and explanations. She let Karos take the lead. He had more authority than her, and the clock was ticking. The longer they spent answering questions in the rain, the greater the kidnappers' head start got.

Once they were back at the embassy, she had questions of her own. Starting with who Kyle the driver was, and why Vykor, who was supposed to be a damned dragon, hadn't done a thing to protect himself or anyone else.

CHAPTER THREE

KAROS QUESTIONED Megan over the short drive back to the embassy, asking her to clarify certain details and trying to build a timeline in his head. He didn't bother asking her to repeat the information she'd given to the police. They'd made her repeat it enough times he had it all committed to memory. More importantly, her story hadn't changed at all, including the details about waking up and finding him standing outside. She was a reliable witness, and he no longer had any doubts about her. At least, not about the attack. He still could not accept the idea that this female -- this small, *human* female, could possibly be his mate. His dragon was mistaken. It had to be.

Megan walked beside him, her bare feet leaving muddy tracks on the pristine marble floor. "Would you like to clean up before we start?" He asked. "Your things were in the back of the vehicle. Someone will already be bringing them to your room."

"I'd love to, but we can't afford the time. The bad guys

already have a head start, and it's getting bigger every second."

"We will find them. This was not a random act. It was carefully orchestrated. Based on the fact you were left alive, we can assume that murder was not the final goal. Whatever it is, they need hostages to make it happen."

She nodded, her features drawn into a thoughtful frown. "That makes sense. But why take humans, a Pyrosian, and a Romaki? Your species are hardly going to make compliant prisoners."

Karos sighed. "Normally, I would agree with you, but Jet is unmated, and Vykor is not..." he trailed off as he searched for the English words that would best explain the other male's situation. "He is unique among my race. He was born without a dragon's spirit."

Megan's stride slowed. "That can happen?"

"It has only happened once. Some of our priests claim it is a sign the Gods are displeased with us. That his existence is a warning that if we do not heed the temples wisdom, more children will be born like him." He shrugged slightly. "I do not believe that, but those that followed the temples into the war did."

"So, he didn't transform because he couldn't? Is that why he didn't do anything to protect himself, or us, during the attack?"

"Vykor has no magic. He is a researcher, not a warrior. There was nothing he could have done to stop what happened today."

Her expression softened. "Lily is the same. I've taught her some basic self-defence, but she's not a fighter, either." Megan's fingers balled into a fist at her side. "And those bastards took her. I'm supposed to protect them both, and I can't do anything for them. This sucks."

He knew exactly how she felt because he felt the same things. Guilt. Frustration. Impatience. On top of all that, he was feeling the first manifestations of the *rux*, the mating fever that came upon all of his race once they scented their mate. For now, it was manageable, and he had every intention of keeping it that way. His dragon had to be wrong about the female. Even if it wasn't, he should be alright so long as he didn't claim her. *No biting. No touching. No problem.*

"We will find them. You should take a moment to clean up and find new footwear. It is going to be a long day. You should be comfortable."

Her mouth set in a stubborn line. "A little mud won't kill me. When I said we were partners, I meant it. Where you go, I go. So, unless you're going to my room to clean up, too, that's not on the agenda."

Being in close quarters with her while she bathed was not a good idea.

"She is ours. Claim her." His dragon stated, its tone frustrated.

"She is not ours."

The beast growled. A basso rumble that rolled through his mind like thunder. *"She is. Why do you deny it?"*

He gritted his teeth. *"Because it cannot be. Not here. Not now. Not her."*

His dragon's only response was sullen silence, which was fine by Karos. He didn't need more distractions right now. He had work to do.

"I'm going to assume by your silence that you're not interested in visiting my room, so where are we going?"

There was a subtle note of disappointment buried beneath Megan's words, and he glanced at her in surprise. She was watching him intently, lips parted, eyes momentarily gleaming with something that made his dragon growl possessively. *"Want. Take. Claim."*

"Be silent."

"Want." The dragon shot back before lapsing into silence again.

Was that what he'd seen in Megan's eyes a moment ago, want? His cock stiffened, and his blood turned to fire at the mere thought she might desire him, and he answered her while he was too distracted by his lust to consider softening his words to something less than a command.

"We will go to your room. We can continue our conversation while you change. You are wet, and your feet must be cold."

She looked ready to argue, but then her eyes narrowed as she took a closer look at his clothing. "We were both standing in the rain for ages. So, how is it that I'm soaked and you're not?" Her gaze raked down his body. "Your shoes aren't even muddy."

"I changed my clothes before we entered the vehicle that drove us here."

"You didn't. I was with you the whole time. I definitely would have noticed if you'd been naked at any point."

"I was never naked. I simply summoned a replacement set of clothing."

"And what happened to your old clothes?" she asked.

"I willed them away. That is part of my magic. A simple but very convenient ability."

"If you willed your clothes away, and then summoned

new ones, you were naked. Maybe only for a second, but you were, and I missed it." She scowled, then flushed. "I'm mean. I didn't notice the change. I uh, I'm usually better at noticing details like that."

"It was very quick. If you like, I can demonstrate."

"You're going to get naked again? Here?"

Every time she said the word, his cock got harder.

"I can summon something for your feet until we reach your room."

"You're kind of fixated on my feet."

"You are leaving a trail of mud behind you." He pointed to the floor back the way they'd come.

She turned to look. "Oops. Didn't think about that. Okay, then. Hocus-pocus me a pair of shoes."

"I am not familiar with that term."

She laughed, a warm, playful sound that flowed over him like a summer breeze. "Make with the magic, please."

He visualized what he wanted and summoned a pair of simple, fur-lined boots to encase her bare feet.

"Shit! Shoes!" She gawked at her feet, lifting one foot, then the other to stare.

"That is what you asked for, is it not?" he teased.

"Well, yeah, but…poof!" She lifted her gaze to meet his. "It's going to take me a bit to get used to the idea that you can just make things happen." She tipped her head to one side. "Which begs the question, why can't you just magic our missing friends back from wherever they are?" She raised a hand and wiggled her fingers in the air between them.

"My magic does not work that way. I can shape the ether into various forms, and I can channel fire in any number of ways, but I cannot do anything like what you are suggesting. Nor do I have any way to track them down. If I could, I would have done so already."

"So, you never need to do laundry, but you can't find our friends. I guess this means we do this the old-fashioned way."

"Indeed. First we find them. Then we save them. Then we crush the ones who did this."

The smile she wore was as fierce as any Romaki warrior's. "Sounds like a plan."

He showed her to her room and stood back as she explored the small but well-appointed space. Her belongings had been transferred to one of the embassy's vehicles while they were giving statements to the police, and her suitcase sat at the end of the bed.

"This is five-star hotel level comfort." She looked back down the hall to the doors that led off in both directions. "Why so many fancy rooms? You can't have that many guests."

He followed her inside and closed the door. "It is the Pyrosians' hope that your species will eventually accept their presence here. When that happens, they will begin hosting Gatherings again."

Megan went over to the bed and unzipped her bag, rifling through the contents as they spoke. "What does that have to do with having so many rooms?"

"As I understand it, once they find their mates and initiate the Spark, things between mates progress rather, uh, quickly."

Megan's eyes widened. "Oh. Yeah. I heard about that." She pulled out a crisply folded shirt, grabbed a pair of jeans, and straightened. "I'm going into the bathroom to wash up and change. I won't be long."

He nodded. "Shall I remove your footwear?"

She paused and glanced back over her shoulder. "Uh, can I keep them for now? They're really comfy, and I hurt my feet trying to kick out that window."

"You are hurt?" He was across the room before he'd finished speaking, standing in front of her, his eyes on her feet. "Show me."

"It's nothing. Just bruised."

He didn't like the idea that she had hidden her damage from him. How could he protect her if he didn't know these things? "You should have said something."

"I'm fine. And the next time my boss tells me to wear heels, I'm going to ignore her."

"Your shoes were not practical," he agreed. "You may continue to use the shoes I conjured for you for as long as you like." He ignored how pleased it made him that she was wearing something he had made for her. She was not his mate. It did not matter if she liked his gifts or not.

"*Ours.*" His dragon muttered at the back of his mind.

"So, uh, I'm going to go change now."

"As you wish." He moved away from her. "We can talk as you do so."

She walked over to the bathroom and went inside, pushing the door almost, but not quite, closed. "I've already told you everything I can remember about the attack."

"You have. But I have not yet told you about what happened here in the minutes before you were rammed."

"Something happened?"

"The protestors out front grew louder and more organized than they have been in weeks. It was enough to bring most of the guards out into the courtyard to keep an eye on them."

The door flew open, revealing her standing there with her shirt only partially buttoned, giving him an eyeful of soft curves and golden skin. "You think they did it on purpose?"

He focused his gaze on the wall to her right and tried to ignore his body's reaction to seeing her partially unclothed. "I do. I think they were instructed to act out so that we'd tell your driver to avoid the front gate and use the side entrance. That's the approach you were on when you were attacked."

She grimaced. "Those sons of bitches. That's how they knew where we'd be."

"And now we know Kyle is working with them, we can assume he gave them the route so they could choose the perfect place to set up the attack. Quiet street. Minimal chance of witnesses. Too far from the embassy for anyone to reach you in time."

"It makes sense. Kyle must have told them we were coming, too. Our arrival was supposed to be a secret." She finally remembered her state of undress, her hands rising to cover herself as she ducked back into the bathroom and pushed the door back into place.

He exhaled sharply and started pacing in an attempt to distract himself. It didn't work. His carefully ordered thoughts and plans on how to find their missing friends were tangled up with lusty thoughts about how it would feel to touch her golden skin, to taste her lips, to press his fangs to her throat and claim her for his own. He slammed his fist into his thigh, using the discomfort to stop the flow of distracting thoughts and images. He didn't have time for this.

"The fever burns."

"This is not the rux. *I have no mate."*

His dragon bellowed in fury, its thoughts strong enough to make him wince. *"There is no I. There is we. We have a mate. Her."*

"I let them die. I do not deserve a mate."

His dragon quieted. *"I miss them. But they are gone. We are not."*

"You still out there?" Megan called a few minutes later.

"Still here. Thinking. They planned this carefully. They have to want something. Why haven't they contacted us to ask for it?"

"Yeah. About that." Megan's words were strained.

"What?" He crossed to the door but didn't open it.

"I found their message."

"Where? What kind of message? What does it say?"

She uttered a ragged, strangled little laugh. "They used me. I'm the message."

The door opened. She stood beyond it, her expression an unreadable mask. The skirt she'd been wearing lay in a heap on the tile floor, and she held jeans in one hand. She wore nothing but a pair of pale pink panties on her lower body, and his cock hardened at the sight of her bare legs.

For a moment, he could think of nothing but how good she looked, but then he saw what she meant, and his lust vanished beneath a surge of cold fury. Words had been scrawled across the skin of her thighs in some kind of thick, black ink. Someone had pushed up her skirt and written on her body, violating her.

He bit back an oath and lifted his gaze to hers. "We will make them pay for this, too."

She nodded, and for a moment, her mask cracked, letting him see the hurt and anger hidden beneath.

"May I take a closer look?"

Another nod. "The right leg looks like a phone number. I think the rest are coordinates. Latitude and longitude, but I'm not sure."

He crouched down to get a better look without crowding her. It appeared she was correct, but when he looked closer, he saw another pair of numbers, one on each leg. The coordinates were labelled with a number one, and the phone number with a two. He pointed, leaving a few inches between his finger and her skin. "It appears they want us to go to the location first, then make contact."

"Then let's go." She took a step toward the door and him.

He set a hand against her mostly bare hip to stop her, and a flash of heat sizzled over his fingers.

"First, we will need to document this and scan the area for any evidence." He tried to keep his tone matter of fact, but he wasn't entirely successful. Whoever had done this to her would pay for touching his mate. No, not his mate. His partner.

"Can you document this? I know it has to be done, but I don't want..." she trailed off.

He understood. She was a warrior and didn't want anyone else to see her vulnerable. "I will do it. No one else needs to be present."

The hard lines of her mouth softened a little. "Thank you. Then, we go save our friends and kick the bad guys' asses, right?"

"Right." He rose and removed his hand from her hip, fighting his desire to stroke his fingers over her skin as he did so. She was focused on what needed to be done. He would do the same.

MEGAN DIDN'T LET anything distract her from her goals. She got the job done and then moved on to whatever came next – until today. Since Karos had arrived in her life, she'd been nothing but distracted, and it was driving her crazy in more ways than one. She was drawn to the rough timbre of his voice, the way his eyes crinkled at the corners when he smiled, and the way his calloused hands felt against her bare skin, which was seven kinds of sinful. She should be focused on getting Hanna and Lily back, but her brain was constantly hijacked by thoughts of the big, magic-wielding alien. *My life has reached a new level of weird.*

She remained undressed until Karos finished documenting the writing on her legs. It should have felt strange, or at least a little embarrassing to be partially naked in front of a total stranger, but there was something about the big, gruff man that put her at ease, even when he was trying to tell her what to do. He might be in charge of embassy security, but she was the one responsible for Hanna and Lily. She'd meant what she'd said. They were partners in this investigation, and they were both invested in making sure the outcome was a good one.

He made a call on the small communicator strapped to his wrist, and a few minutes later a young male in a Pyrosian military uniform arrived at the door. He handed Karos a few items, spoke briefly to him in a language she didn't understand, thumped a hand to his chest in some kind of salute, and departed.

She watched the interaction from the comfort of her massive bed. She was sitting on the bed, her feet, back in the soft boots he'd conjured for her, dangling over the edge of the mattress. The room was cold enough she should have felt chilled, but she didn't. In fact, she felt uncomfortably warm. She glanced down at her legs again.

She'd been used. Violated. Treated like an object, a way to convey a message to the aliens at the embassy. She didn't matter to them. They'd used her and then left her unconscious in the open limo, vulnerable and alone.

She gritted her teeth and resisted the urge to scrub her hands over the writing on her skin. It wouldn't come off, and she'd destroy any potential evidence if she touched it.

When she looked up again, Karos was standing a few feet away, holding several items in his big hands. He watched her with concern in his strange golden eyes, and she wanted to reach for him and claim what comfort she could from his arms. Instead, she gave him what she hoped was a confident smile and gestured to the objects he carried. "What are those?"

He set them down on the bed as he named each one. "An image recorder, a device that will scan for fingerprints or forensic evidence, and something that can process and identify any genetic material we find and compare it to all known databases."

She eyed the collection of technology. None of it looked much different than her cell phone. "Those are some interesting toys. I would've loved having access to tech like that when I worked as a mountie."

"I believe this technology is now being offered to law

enforcement departments all over your planet." He held up the gizmo he'd called an image recorder. "Do I have your permission?"

She nodded and scooted back on the bed so that her legs were stretched out in front of her. He took more than a dozen pictures, capturing the writing from various angles. He had her part her legs slightly for the last few, and her cheeks were burning by the time he was finished.

"I know this isn't pleasant for you, but I will do my best to get this over with as quickly as possible. I have my team identifying the coordinates and determining a safe approach. They should be done by the time we join them."

"I'm okay. I know this needs to be done."

Next, he set down the imager and picked up the scanner. He flicked a switch, and it emitted a pale green glow. He started to move it up his hand to demonstrate how it worked, then stopped when he realized he was still wearing his jacket. One second it was there, the next it was gone, revealing the dark grey, short-sleeved shirt he wore beneath.

"It won't hurt at all." He said, running it up his newly bared and nicely muscled arm.

"Did you just magic away your jacket?" she asked, her eyes still on his perfectly sculpted forearm.

"It was in my way." He held the device over her legs. "May I scan you?"

She nodded affirmatively. "You may. And remind me to never get in your way, Big Red."

His brows rose. "What did you call me?"

"Big Red. It just kind of slipped out."

"It is not inaccurate. I am both big, and red-haired." He smiled a little as he activated the device and ran it slowly over her legs. There was nothing but a faint tingling sensation as it passed over her.

She wasn't sure what to say to that without getting herself in trouble. Did aliens do double *entendres*?

It didn't take him long to finish scanning her. Once he was done, she returned to the bathroom, turned the hot water on, and took a few minutes to try and scrub off the writing on her skin. She knew it wouldn't all come off, but she felt better for having tried. Her skin stung by the time she was done, the lines slightly faded on her now reddened skin. She finished dressing, finger combed her hair back into place, picked her skirt up, and re-entered the main room.

"We should scan this, too," she said.

Karos raised his head and accepted the item with a nod. "Good thinking. The scan detected several traces of cellular residue on your legs."

"What are the odds of the suspect being in a database?"

"If they are staff, the odds are very good. If not..." He shrugged.

"You think Kyle wasn't the only traitor?"

"I think it would be best not to make any assumptions. Kyle fooled us. There might be others." He held her skirt by the waistband and started sweeping the fabric in slow, deliberate motions.

"You said this place would be safe. If there are others, none of us are safe."

He looked up, his golden eyes bright as they stared into hers. "Once we are done here, we will make a stop at the armoury before we go to the command center. If this place is not safe, then we will make it so."

She grinned. "Did you just offer to arm me? You keep

sweet-talking me like this Big Red, you and I might have to grab a drink when this is all over."

He dropped his gaze back to the device in his hand without speaking, but she thought she heard him growl under his breath. The barely-there sound made her tingle in all the right places. She'd never had a thing for alpha types before. *And I don't have one now. Get your head in the game.*

CHAPTER FOUR

KAROS LED Megan to the lower floors of the embassy. Down here, the elegant tile and artwork had been replaced with simple flooring and a labyrinth of non-descript hallways that stretched out in all directions. They walked in silence, both of them deep in thought about what came next.

The scan of the human female's garment produced a fingerprint. It only took a few seconds to identify it as Kyle McLeod's. Once he knew that, he compared the other samples he'd recovered to Kyle's profile and got a hit. He'd been planning on making Kyle pay for his treachery, but now he would make sure the lying *traxyn* suffered for what he'd done to Megan.

"We hurt him," his dragon declared.

"We will," he promised the beast.

"Unless she finds him first. Our mate is fierce," the dragon's words were full of approval.

As promised, they'd stopped at the armoury along the way, and Megan was now outfitted with a mixture of human and Romaki weaponry. She would have taken one of everything in inventory if she could have found a way to carry it all. She'd asked for the specifications of every weapon she didn't recognize and made her preliminary choices, setting the items aside until they filled an entire table. He'd watched in amusement as she'd made her final selections and put the rest back with obvious reluctance.

She *was* fierce. Loyal, too. With courage and strength that rivalled that of any Romaki warrior.

"Tali would have liked her," his dragon said softly.

"She would have." Tali. He didn't think about her often. It hurt less that way. To remember her, he had to remember the fact he hadn't been there the day she'd died. After a lifetime of guarding each other's backs, he'd failed her. The scars on his back ached, reminding him of the day it happened. If he'd been with her, she'd still be alive.

"Or we'd be buried beside her."

It was not the first time they'd had this conversation. While the dragon spirit was part of him, it wasn't all of him. It was the more primal part of his nature, a creature driven by instincts, including survival. It didn't understand guilt or remorse.

He envied its ignorance.

They reached the door of the command center. They were deep underground in an area that was more bunker than office building. This area was prone to earthquakes, and the embassy had been built to withstand anything that the planet, or the beings that inhabited it, could throw at it.

As the doors opened on a large room full of uniformed staff and a wide array of technology, Megan uttered a low whistle. "I feel like I'm on the bridge of the *USS Enterprise*."

He had been encouraged to view a large amount of the human's entertainment programming and recognized her *Star Trek* reference. He didn't mention that the bridge of an actual spaceship was far more cramped and utilitarian than the room they entered. Everything here was still relatively new, and they had ample space for a generous layout. "This place houses a combination of Pyrosian and Romaki technology, far more advanced than what your species has."

"For now. With help from both of your species, we're catching up fast."

He reached out and tapped the grip of the sidearm she'd selected from the armoury. "There are some technologies your species isn't ready for yet. I believe you are the first human to carry that weapon." He gave her a small smile. "Just remember that unlike *Star Trek's* weaponry, that one does not have a stun setting."

She bared her teeth in a feral smile and lowered her voice so only he could hear her response. "Good. The ones I plan on shooting don't deserve to be stunned."

They entered, and everyone inside turned to look their way before returning to their tasks. There were more than half a dozen beings present, most of them viewing monitors or three-dimensional displays of the city. They'd been tasked with the daunting job of locating Jet, Vykor, and the two missing humans in a city of over two million beings. While there were some humans on the embassy staff, only one of them had access to this area: Eva Amarin.

Eva's normally sunny smile was missing as she crossed the room to meet them, but even the small smile she offered Megan was enough to show her dimples.

"You must be Megan. I'm Eva. I'm sorry about what

happened to your companions. We're doing all we can to find them, and our friends," she said in English.

"Thank you. I wasn't sure at first, but now I believe that your people are the best chance Hanna and Lily have of being rescued." Megan smiled back and relaxed slightly.

Eva had that effect on everyone. The small blonde female exuded kindness and acceptance, along with a dizzying amount of energy when the situation required it.

"You had doubts?" Eva's gold eyes widened. "About us?"

"It was your driver who gassed us. And Vykor didn't do anything to help." Megan shrugged apologetically. "Karos explained to me about Vykor. I understand now, but when I first came to I was disoriented, upset, and…" She glanced up at him and smiled. "Then there was this big, bossy jerk standing outside the limo barking orders at me."

Eva giggled and lowered her voice to a stage whisper. "He does that a lot."

Keth joined them, his arm sliding around his mate's waist. "What have I told you about teasing the dragon, *seska*?"

Eva looked up at her mate with an expression of adoration so pure it made Karos' heart ache. "You said I shouldn't mess in the affairs of dragons, because humans are crunchy and taste good with ketchup."

Megan snickered.

"I do not eat beings. That would be disgusting." Karos grumbled. "Nor would I ever consider doing you harm, Eva. You know this, which is why you know it is safe to tease me."

"Wait. Dragons don't eat people? What about all the legends about dragons snacking on knights and flying off with virgins?" Megan asked.

"If I were hungry, I'd conjure food. I have no need to eat my enemies. It's easier to simply turn them to ash." He grinned, deliberately flashing his fangs.

"And the virgins?" Megan asked, her lips curved in a bare hint of a smile.

"Company, of course. Even the grumpiest of dragons likes someone to uh…talk to." Keth held out his hand to Megan in greeting. "I'm Keth. Eva and I manage the embassy, which means that what happened today is my fault. I am truly sorry."

Karos shook his head. "The fault was mine. I'm in charge of security." The guilt he felt would only ease once this ordeal was over and everyone was returned safely.

"And I should have done more to protect everyone when the attack started." Megan straightened up and squared her shoulders. "Now that we've established that we're all feeling guilty, how are we going to get them back?"

"By any means necessary," Karos stated.

"Good attitude, Big Red, but maybe a few more details?" she retorted.

Keth chuckled. "Big Red? Really?"

"It is accurate enough." Karos ignored the Pyrosian's amusement and held out his hand to Megan. "Your device had a tracking program. What was it tracking? Perhaps we can replicate it and amplify the signal."

She pulled out her phone and handed it to him. "It can track their phones or the tracking devices they wear as jewellery. It's been scanning for a signal since the limo, though, and so far, nothing."

"Your people are wearing trackers? That's ingenious. I should implement a similar protocol for the embassy staff."

"Hanna's is built into a pendant, and Lily's is a charm on her bracelet. I had them made for trips to some of the more dangerous areas we travel in."

Karos handed the phone to Eva, who took it over one of the Pyrosian computer techs. Then, he turned to Keth. "How far away are the coordinates we were given? How long will it take to get there?"

Keth grimaced. "Not long. In fact, I've already dispatched a team to retrieve it."

"What? No? I want to be part of this, damn it," Megan interjected.

Karos agreed with her. "Security is my job, not yours."

"Which is why I want you both here. I'm not risking either of you on what should be a delivery run." Keth pointed to a massive monitor that took up most of one wall. "Attin, Bring up the live feed."

One of the Pyrosian males nodded in acknowledgment. "Yes, sir."

Video feeds appeared on the monitor in neat rows. Karos recognized the area immediately. "Why are we looking at security footage from the camera by the side gate?" he asked.

"Because those coordinates are for a spot just north of the gate." Keth leaned over Attin, touched the monitor, and the image on the large screen zoomed in on a small box set on the ground on the far side of the alley.

"That wasn't there before." Karos took a long look at

the object. It wasn't large, maybe thirty centimetres long with a fitted lid. The cardboard appeared to be damp, but not soaking wet. It hadn't been out in the rain for long.

"It was dropped forty-two minutes ago, while you were on your way back here," Keth said.

"Dropped?" Megan asked. "Who dropped it off? Are you running facial recognition?"

"It was delivered via drone." Keth's tone turned sour and he called up another feed, adding it to the large monitor. This one clearly showed a small drone flying into the alley and releasing the box, letting it fall several meters to the ground before zipping off again.

"I'm getting tired of being three steps behind these jerks," Megan muttered.

"As am I." Karos rumbled in agreement. "Where is the security team?"

"They are standing by near the gate. They've scanned the container and done what we could to ensure there's nothing dangerous inside."

"What about biological matter?" Megan's voice held a sharp edge.

"There were no weapons present. Biological, chemical, or otherwise," Keth said.

"That's not what I meant. Sometimes humans deliver a body part, a finger or an ear, for example, to convey the seriousness of the threat to the ones who were taken."

Eva made a small, horrified sound. "They wouldn't do that. Would they?"

Keth drew his mate in closer to his side. "There was nothing like that inside the container."

Megan exhaled softly. "Good."

"I want to know what *is* in that box." Karos glanced

over at Attin. "Open a channel to the security team for me?"

"Yes, sir." Attin nodded when the link was established.

"Security team. This is Karos Zattar, your commanding officer. Identify yourselves."

One by one, the six members of the team announced themselves. Keth had chosen well. The six were all steadfast males with good instincts and advanced training. He was still getting used to overseeing teams that had little or no females. His species had their share of problems, but at least they didn't have to deal with the prospect of dying out because of a lack of mates.

"Everything's ready on our end. Give us the word, and we'll retrieve the package, sir," Toran stated.

"Activate your personal feed and proceed."

Two seconds later, another feed appeared on the monitor, this one from Toran's perspective. The room stilled. Silent tension crept over everyone as they watched the team approach. It didn't matter how many scans they'd done, the males were taking a serious risk, and everyone knew it.

Beside him, Megan watched, her upper body leaning forward as Toran leaned down and removed the top of the box. Nothing happened. There was a collective breath as everyone relaxed slightly.

"There appear to be five communication devices. One Pyrosian, one Romaki, and three human cell phones. Only one of the cell phones is intact, sir. The others have been destroyed."

Toran flipped over the lid and showed them the instructions on the underside.

Make contact within ten minutes of opening the package. The contact information is on Richards. We are watching.

"Bring the package and the contents into the courtyard. I'll meet you there." Karos turned on his heel, making straight for the door.

Megan was only half a step behind him. "They destroyed their phones. That's why we couldn't track them that way."

"And the third device is how they want us to communicate with them," he continued, resisting the sudden urge to reach back for her hand and bring her in close to his side – where she belonged.

"I hate this. They've got us dancing to their tune. We're never going to get ahead of them like this."

"We will find a way."

"We better. Our friends' lives depend on it."

Karos gave her a curt nod and kept walking. He wanted to comfort her, to hold her and assure her that they'd find a way to make this right. The Gods must be testing him. Why else would they do this him in the middle of a crisis? He still didn't believe she was his mate, but he couldn't ignore her effect on him. She was desirable, beautiful, courageous, and a distraction he couldn't allow

---

MEGAN CAUGHT HERSELF OGLING KAROS' ass as he walked ahead of her. For a mature man, he was in amazing shape. If it weren't for the silver in his hair and the lines around his eyes, she'd put him in his thirties, tops. Then again, his species was supposed to live for centuries. "How old are you?"

He glanced back at her in surprise. "In Earth years? A little over two hundred. Why?"

She nearly stumbled, too surprised to pay attention to what her feet were doing. He was two hundred years old? It was hard to imagine living that long. Or looking that good after two centuries. "Just curious. You seemed older than most of the others back there, but I've only met one other Romaki, so I don't have much to go on."

"Vykor is young. Less than a hundred of your years." They reached the elevator and he pressed the call button. "How old are you?"

"Normally I'd refuse to answer that question, but since I asked you first..." She shrugged. "I'll be forty next month. Not young anymore."

"You have lived long enough to attain experience and wisdom." His golden eyes gleamed as he looked her over. "You should be proud of your age and all you have accomplished. Not every warrior lives as long as we have."

There was something in his tone that made her ask another question before her brain could catch up to her mouth. "Who did you lose?"

His eyes darkened but he didn't say anything until the elevator arrived. He gestured for her to go first, then joined her inside. When the door closed, he answered, his voice dull and flat. "A friend. She died fighting for the future of our planet. A future she will never get to see for herself."

Megan reached up and set her hand on his shoulder. "I'm sorry."

He looked down at her hand then covered it with his own for a moment. "Thank you."

His gaze moved to her face, their eyes locking. She didn't look away, and neither did he. Heart pounding. Mouth dry. She lifted her other hand to reach for him, then stopped. What the hell was she doing?

He caught her hand in his, drew her in close, and bowed his head to brush a slow kiss over her mouth. Heat flared deep inside her, and she rose on her toes to kiss him back. Karos uttered a low growl that turned her brain to mush and sent a rush of raw lust coursing through her veins.

For one searing moment she forgot about everything but him. All her fears, guilt, and worry vanished in a firestorm that reached her very soul. She drank in the essence of him. His warmth. His strength. The possessive slant of his mouth as it laid claim to hers. She breathed in his scent, a subtle blend of soap and something wilder, like the air after a storm.

The next thing she knew, the elevator stopped and the doors opened. They both stepped back at the same time, their hands releasing to fall back to their sides. Neither of them said a word as they exited the space, and the silence stretched between them as they walked the rest of the way to the outer doors.

As he opened the door he paused and looked back at her. "I should apolo—"

She cut him off with a slash of her hand. "Don't you dare."

"But…"

"It happened. I'm not sorry it did. Are you?" She watched and waited, her heart slamming against her ribs as she waited for him to make his choice. After that kiss, there was no going back for her. Crazy or not. She wanted more. But did he?

He frowned. His mouth opening and closing several times before he finally shook his head. "We don't have time for this right now."

"You kissed me. You don't get to do that and then tell me we don't have time to talk about it."

That's when she remembered they were meeting the security team outside. She looked past the door and saw six uniformed men staring at the two of them with expressions that ranged from bemusement to outright surprise. *Wonderful.*

Karos glanced outside, then back to her. "I do not regret kissing you. I do regret the timing."

She considered that for a second. The timing sucked. No argument there. "Fair enough. First, we rescue our friends, and then you and I are going to revisit this conversation."

"As you wish."

Toran raised a brow at Karos as they stepped into the rain-soaked courtyard and said something in what she assumed was either Pyrosian or Romaki. She wasn't fluent in either language, and she only heard one word clearly. *Bakkia.*

"Do I want to know what he said?" she asked Karos quietly as they joined the others. The rain had stopped, but the clouds overhead were still an ugly dark grey and the wind swirled around the courtyard, cold enough to make her shiver.

Toran's eyes widened slightly. "I apologize. I thought all the humans working at the embassy had been given cognitive augmentation to allow them to speak our languages."

"I'm not embassy staff." She cocked her head. "So, what did you say?"

Grinning now, Toran nodded to Karos. "I said you were a *bakkia*. A lovely flower well protected by thorns."

She borrowed one of Karos' phrases. "It is not an inaccurate description."

Karos chuckled. "Toran, this is Megan Richards. Megan, this is Guardsman Toran Kantos."

Megan started to offer her hand to the big Pyrosian, but stopped when she noticed his eyes weren't gold. Protocol dictated that unclaimed Pyrosians refrain from physical contact while on duty. No sudden onset of the Spark that way. She withdrew her hand, and Toran gave her a smile and an understanding nod.

"Where's the package?" Karos asked.

Another Pyrosian appeared and handed it to Karos. "We scanned the contents and the container already. There's nothing we can use to identify the ones who did this, sir."

"What about tracing the call we're about to make?" Megan asked.

Karos shook his head. "There's not enough time to set it up. They'll do what they can downstairs, and I'll record everything so we can go over it later." He checked the communicator on his wrist. "Less than two minutes left."

"Then we better make the call." She held out her hand. "May I? I've had some training in hostage negotiations."

Karos only hesitated for a second before pulling the working phone out of the box and handing it to her.

"Thank you." She activated the phone, set it to speaker

mode so everyone could listen in, and dialled the number from memory. It was etched into her mind, and she'd probably go to her grave remembering every digit.

The ring tone sounded three times before someone answered. "You found our message." A male voice. Steady. Confident. No accent. Not markedly young or old.

"I did. Who am I speaking to?" she asked, holding the phone so that her voice would carry clearly, but the others could hear what was being said.

"The man calling the shots. You must be Ms. Richards."

"It is. Now you know my name. May I have yours?" It wasn't easy to stay polite and calm. She wanted to tell him exactly what she planned on doing to him once he was caught. She wanted to scream, or demand he let her talk to Hanna and Lily. Instead, she gripped the phone tighter and kept talking.

"You don't need to know my name. All you need to know is what I expect to happen. Have one of those alien freaks standing with you take notes, Ms. Richards. I won't repeat myself."

Karos and the others looked around, trying to spot whoever, or whatever was spying on them. She didn't look up. She needed to stay focused. "I'm ready. What are your demands?"

"A trade. A life for a life. You release two prisoners to me, and I'll release mine to you."

"Unhurt?"

The speaker paused for several long, painful seconds. "That depends on you and the alien invaders."

"I want to speak to Hanna Dewan."

"We don't always get what we want in life. I know I didn't. If I had, my country, my *world*, wouldn't be overrun with arrogant aliens who think they can take whatever they want. Our land. Our resources. Our women. It's going to stop. We're not going down without a fight. This is our world, and we're taking it back." There was no mistaking the sincerity of the man's crazy. He believed the garbage he was spewing. He was a zealot. A true believer. And that made him all kinds of dangerous.

She glanced up at Karos and he met her gaze. Understanding passed between them. He flashed his fangs at her. It was a swift but ferocious expression that told her he knew what this man was. He knew, and he planned on taking him down anyway.

Good. So did she.

"What are the names of the prisoners you want released?" She already had a good idea who it was, and Satan would be ice skating to work before the leader of the Humanity First movement got to breathe free air again.

"Justin Kines and Remy Russell." The man stated. "I know this will take some time. You have until noon tomorrow morning to arrange for their release. When everything is in order, call this number again and I'll give you your next instructions."

"Not until I know that all four hostages are alive." She replied firmly.

"You are not controlling this narrative, Ms. Richards. Do as your told."

"I need—" The line went dead. "Dammit."

Karos tapped his wrist, reminding her that he'd been recording everything. "We need to get inside. I want to get a better look at the contents of the box."

"So do I."

Karos handed the active phone to Toran. "Take this

downstairs. I've already sent a copy of the recording to them. I don't think they'll find anything, but we have to try. We will join you there shortly."

The Pyrosian nodded once, turned on his heel, and jogged to the door. The rest of the team took up positions around her and Karos. It was the first time she'd been the protectee instead of the protector, and it felt more than a little strange.

They stayed with them until they reached the door, opening it for them and holding position until she and Karos were both safely inside.

"Do you have posts to report to?" Karos asked.

The males nodded.

"Then get to them. Good job."

"Thank you," she added as they separated and headed off in all directions.

Karos headed back the way they'd come, but she stopped him with a touch. "Before we go any farther, I need to see what's in there."

He hesitated, then handed her the box. "Be quick."

She held the package in the crook of her arm and sorted carefully through the contents. She didn't bother looking at the two alien devices. She had no way of knowing how they worked. The phones though... The phones had been destroyed. Screens cracked. Their casings broken. When she lifted one from the box a dribble of water flowed out of it, and a quick check confirmed they'd removed the sim cards, too. She found those in the bottom of the box, both of them snapped in two, along with something none of the others had noticed – A figure-eight shaped gold pendant that should have had a red gem set in the lower loop. The gem was gone. Her stomach twisted into a new set of knots as she plucked the pendant out and held it up for Karos to see.

"This is Hanna's. There was a gem set into it. Inside the gem was a transponder."

Karos frowned. "They took it out? How would they know to do that?"

She dropped the pendant back into the box and lowered her hand before he could notice the way it shook. "Either they checked her for bugs and found it that way, or…"

"Or someone told them what to look for," he finished for her.

Doubts sank needle sharp into her guts and started pumping its poison into her, making her question everything. "I can't believe that. The only ones that knew about the transponders were me, Hanna, and Lily."

Karos searched the box. "You said she had a transponder too. A charm, right?" He asked without looking up.

She already knew what he saw. Lily's transponder wasn't there. She didn't know what that meant. Not yet. But Kyle might not have been the only insider. "I'm going to need access to a computer for a few hours. There are a few details I need to check."

He nodded and didn't comment further. She was grateful for his silence.

"We shall bring it all to the command center and begin our investigation. While we do that, Keth can call the Canadian government and let them know what's happened. We're going to need their cooperation."

"You think they're going to agree to release Kines and

Russell?" The idea sickened her, but so did the thought of never seeing her friends again.

"I think we need to be prepared for all possibilities."

And with that, they set off down the hallway, Karos a silent, steady presence at her side.

CHAPTER FIVE

KAROS KNEW he needed sleep in order to function at his best, but nothing he did brought him any respite. The *rux* made it impossible to think for long, but when he could, he tried to plan for every contingency he could think of. Then the mating fever would flare up again, and he'd be driven mad with lust and thoughts of Megan. There was no denying the truth anymore. He was under the thrall of the *rux*, and it was getting stronger with every breath he took. Only the fact he hadn't claimed her allowed him to keep some semblance of control, but he was running out of time.

It had been well after midnight when he and Megan had parted company at her door. She'd spent much of the evening investigating anything that might indicate her friend had betrayed her. She hadn't found anything, but he knew she still harboured concerns, along with a heavy dose of guilt for even considering that Lily was working for the Humanity First movement.

She had looked as tired and worried as he felt, and despite copious amounts of stimulant-laced beverages, she was swaying on her feet by the time they reached her room. It had taken all his will power not to lift her into his arms and carry her down the last stretch of hallway, and by the time he bade her goodnight, his hands itched with the need to touch her. To comfort her.

Tomorrow he would have to tell Keth what was going on so the Pyrosian could arrange for someone else to take over, should the need arise. Then, he would have to find a way to tell Megan she was his *sadina*, his mate. Somehow, he didn't think she would be pleased to hear it. Not if it meant leaving the rescue of her friends to someone else. He knew exactly how she felt.

After more than an hour of trying to rest, he gave up the fight and got out of bed again. He dressed quickly, donning a pair of loose-fitting pants and a sleeveless shirt. His skin was so hot he couldn't tolerate more clothing than that. He even left his shoes off and walked barefoot from his rooms down to the gymnasium and training area set up on one of the lower floors.

He had the place to himself and quickly settled into his usual routine, limbering up, and then taking out his frustrations on the heavy bag set up in one corner of the space. The familiar pattern of strikes, punches, and kicks helped clear his mind a bit, though it did little to ease his physical state. He was still overheating, and he stripped off his shirt, tossing it into a corner without losing the rhythm of his attacks.

He needed to find his focus, but the only clear thoughts he had were about Megan. Her smile. Her strength. The way her eyes shifted colours depending on the light. The way she'd tasted… Holy flames of Daga, just thinking about that one, too-brief kiss they'd shared was enough to set his blood on fire.

His next punch nearly tore through the heavy fabric bag. The support beam shuddered and groaned at the abuse, and he took a step back, lowering his hands and sucking in a deep breath. Destroying the equipment wouldn't help matters.

The bag was still swinging wildly when the door slid open and someone else entered the gym. Her scent wrapped around him like a physical caress, and he knew without looking that Megan was there.

"You couldn't sleep either, huh?" she asked.

Just hearing her voice turned him to stone, and he kept his back turned as he willed his errant biology to behave. It didn't work. "I thought some exercise might help me settle down, but it has failed to do so."

"Maybe you're doing the wrong kind of exercising."

There was no ignoring the undertone to her words, a low, sultry note that made his dragon lunge against the confines of his mind. *"Claim. Keep. Ours!"*

He spun around to face her, drinking in the sight of her standing on the mats wearing a pair of red leggings and a black tank-top that skimmed over her curves. "You had something else in mind?"

Her eyes widened, and a blush rose up her throat and stained her cheeks. "I can't believe I said that. I thought maybe we could spar or something, but it came out all wrong." she shook her head. "I don't know what the hell is wrong with me today."

He knew exactly what was wrong. The *rux*. He wasn't sure how to tell her, though. The Pyrosians were on Earth looking for their true mates. The humans knew about that process, but no one had considered the possibility that the handful of Romaki on the planet would find their mates here, too. At least, he hadn't considered it. He didn't deserve a mate. He couldn't be trusted to protect one.

Megan sighed. "Is brooding silence your way of telling me I should find somewhere else to be?"

"No. Don't go." He stepped toward her, one hand already reaching for her before he realized what he was doing. He wanted to touch her so badly it was a physical pain.

"You're sure?"

"I am certain. It has been a trying day and my mind is full of distracting thoughts. I would be happy to spar with you. Maybe it will give us both what we need." And maybe if she hit him a few times, he'd stop speaking in words that held more than one meaning. The *rux* was twisting his mind, and his tongue.

She raised an eyebrow at him, her lips curving into a ghost of a smile. "Maybe."

He waited for her to warm up, trying not to stare as she stretched and contorted her body in interesting ways. Once she was done, he joined her in the middle of the mats and waited for her to make the first move.

"Ready?" she asked.

"Ready."

He barely had time to utter the word before she came at him. He expected her to throw a punch or kick, but instead, she moved in close and grappled with him, using her lower center of gravity to her advantage. He grunted in surprise and reacted, untangling himself from her and taking two long steps backward so she had to come at him again.

This time, he was ready, and when she moved in close, he responded with a quick series of strikes that forced her to go on the defensive. Neither of them fought at full strength, but each attack and counter was real enough to demand his full attention. Since part of his mind was distracted by Megan, that meant he made mistakes. Fortunately, so did she. A countermove that was a second slow. A kick that missed its target by a finger's breadth. She was good, but he could sense her frustration growing with every error. Just like his was.

"Where did you learn to fight?" He asked as they moved. He'd been learning what he could of the various human martial arts, but her style wasn't one he knew. Or more likely, it was a combination of several, blended into something unique to her.

"A few places. My father was in the navy when he was younger, and he taught me to protect myself. Later, I signed on with the Bold Eagle program." She threw a punch that he should have blocked, but his hand came up a little to slow to deflect it completely.

"What's that?"

"A military recruiting program for aboriginal Canadians. Ranger training, mostly. In the end, I went with the RCMP instead. I wanted to make a difference, and I thought law enforcement was a better fit."

"Was it?" He understood the desire to do something meaningful with one's life. That was why he'd joined the military, too.

"For a while. But as you might have noticed, I'm not

really good at taking orders. I was assigned to protect Hanna while she was on a trip with a number of other dignitaries from Canada. She offered me a job. I took it. I've been with her ever since."

Loyalty. That was another thing they had in common. The more he got to know Megan, the easier it became to accept that she was his mate. The Gods had terrible timing, but he was running out of reasons to deny she was meant for him... and he for her.

They continued their dance, coming at each other harder now. She was glowing with exertion, breathing hard, a smile on her lips. Gods, she was beautiful. Their eyes locked and for a moment she just stared at him, the fierce fire in her eyes turning into something else, something more. Desire.

"*Ours,*" his dragon howled, and he closed in on her, wrapping her in his arms and lifting her so he could seal her mouth with a kiss.

She stiffened for a moment, and then softened into his arms, her legs wrapping around his waist as he walked her over to the nearest wall and pressed her against it. A low moan rose from her throat, his hands cupping the soft globes of her ass as he ground himself between her legs, his tongue twining with hers.

He held her against the wall with his hips, using one hand to tear at her clothes as their kisses deepened, the scent and taste and feel of her making him feel like he was drowning in a sea of flames. With the last of his will power he tore his mouth from hers and looked down at her. "Do I have your permission, Megan? I want you, but only if this is what you want, too."

She took a ragged breath and framed his face with her

hands. Her lips were swollen with his kisses, her eyes heavy-lidded and gleaming with arousal. "I want this, too. Whatever this is, I want it badly."

He bowed his head so their foreheads touched and stared into her eyes. "This is the *rux*."

"What's that?"

He drew in a breath, then uttered words he never imagined he'd say. "You are my mate, Megan Richards. You are *mine*."

Pleasure and need had fogged her brain so badly it took her a few seconds for his words to sink in. The moment they did, she dropped her hands to his shoulders and pushed him back a few inches. "Whoa. I'm your mate? Since when? How?"

He lowered her to the floor, letting her slide down his body so that she felt every hard inch of him on her way down. "My dragon knew from the moment we met. I refused to believe it at first. He's going to be incredibly smug about this."

"Your dragon is going to be smug? Aren't you the same thing –things?" She shook her head, trying to make sense of everything.

"We are two parts of the same whole, though our dragon is the manifestation of our deepest instincts and desires. Sometimes, we disagree."

"Wait, you argue with yourself. Do you lose much?" She knew she was deliberately ignoring what he'd said about being mates, but she wasn't ready to deal with that.

Not yet. Maybe not ever, but somehow, she doubted denial was going to be an option.

"When my dragon first emerged, I lost a few times. I was almost as wild and impulsive as he was. It hasn't been like that for more than a century, though." He lifted his free hand to stroke her hair back from her face. "Not until I met you."

"And this *rux* thing…it's why you kissed me earlier?"

"The *rux* is a mating fever. It happens when we find the one we are destined for. I kissed you because I desired you, but the *rux* was part of it, yes."

"And it means we're mates? Forever?"

"Forever." He nodded. "You are my *sadina*. Will be together from now until the moment of our deaths. That is the way of things with my people."

That definitely sounded permanent, which was a problem. She was not the kind of person who did permanent very well. She liked change. Travel. New challenges. She fought a rising tide of panic and asked deflected again, "*Sadina*?"

"It's how we say mate in my language. It's a title as well as a word. You are destined to be my *sadina*, and I will be your *sodono*."

"Uh huh. So, this is how it is for your species, but what about mine? We don't do mating fevers and destiny. Well, not outside of Hollywood movies and romance novels, which are awesome, but not exactly grounded in reality."

"I don't know. There's only been one other mating like this. Prince Radek of the Snow Dragon Clan found his mate here on Earth, too."

"And she just went with it? Poof, she's a dragon's girlfriend living on another planet." She remembered hearing the story, but never in a million years had she considered it could happen to her.

He chuckled. "I believe it took her some time to adjust, but yes, she is mated to Prince Radek."

"And what if I don't want to be mated?"

His voice lowered to a low rumble. "We have no choice in this. The Gods have made their decision. We must abide by it." His thumb traced over her lower lip. "I wasn't prepared for you, either. But now I have you, there is not a force in the universe that could make me give you up."

"Even if I said no?" Every cell in her body was screaming yes, but as much as she wanted him, she needed to know she had some choice. Destiny be damned.

He stiffened. "If you decline, I will give you all the time I can, but the *rux*…it will grow stronger as time passes, and we have already been in its thrall for hours."

"Stronger?" She already felt like her libido had been dialled up to eleven. "For how long?"

"Days. Three or four. It's impossible to know."

"But the others. We have to find them."

"We will. I don't know how, but we'll find a way. The *rux* will fog our minds, but not all the time. We will manage."

She took a slow breath and tried to untangle her brain from the needs of her body. She wanted him. She really, really wanted him. She liked him, too. But love? Forever? She couldn't deal with that right now. "If we sleep together, will it get easier to think clearly?"

He nodded slowly. "For a time. Then the *rux* will build again." His lips turned up into a slow, sexy smile. "But to be clear, I do not intend for either of us to do much sleeping."

That smile melted her brain and made her heart race. She already knew her answer. It wasn't the most rational decision she'd ever made, but the logic worked well enough. For once, she could have what she wanted without feeling like she'd abandoned her duty, and what she wanted, was him. "Then, my answer is yes. Just for tonight, though. We'll have to figure out the rest later."

"But for tonight, you belong to me." His words ended on a growl that made her toes curl, and then his mouth was on hers. His kiss was searing, igniting a firestorm of passion that threatened to consume her. She closed her eyes and let it happen.

Strong hands fisted her shirt and she waited for the sound of tearing fabric, but instead he muttered a single word and her clothing vanished. Her bare skin pressed to the wall behind her, the cool air of the gym washing her overheated flesh like a winter wind.

She placed her hands on his hips and tugged at the waistband of his pants in silent encouragement. It melted away beneath her fingers. She ran her hands over him, exploring his body inch by hungry inch.

When he finally raised his head and broke the kiss, she opened her eyes and got her first look at him. Naked. Hard. His golden eyes gleamed with a hunger that stole her breath and made her heart pound. His cock was caught between them. She felt the thickness of it, along with several hard, raised ridges that intrigued her. What would that feel like when he took her? She couldn't wait to find out.

"Wow." It wasn't the most flattering of comments, but her brain wasn't working very well.

"Wow, indeed." Karos cupped her face in his large

hands, leaning in to kiss her gently before letting his gaze drift over her. "Bless Daga and Solun for gifting me with a goddess of my own."

"Pretty sure you're the god here, mister I can turn into a dragon and make with the magical mojo at will. And a very sexy one at that."

Heat flared in his golden eyes as he sank to his knees in front of her, brushing hungry kisses to her stomach, moving lower with every kiss. She buried her hands in his dark red hair, steadying herself against the onslaught of sensation his touch unleashed.

Without a word, he slid a hand between her legs, coaxing her to widen her stance. She moved her legs apart, trying to ignore the sudden sense of vulnerability that came with her new position. Vulnerable. Open. Directly in front of the door… *Shit*.

"We need to stop. The door. Someone could walk in and see…a lot more than I'm comfortable with."

His expression darkened, and for a second she thought he was going to protest. "I should have thought of that. I am sorry, *sadina*." He held out a hand to the door and uttered a guttural sound that only vaguely sounded like language at all. A second later, the access panel beside the door sizzled, sparked, and went dead. "No one is coming through that door, now."

"What did you do?" she asked, drawing out the words.

He grinned, the playful expression making him look like much younger man. "Magical mojo."

She opened her mouth to reply, but her words died unspoken as he reached between her thighs and slid a thick finger into her folds, stroking directly over her clit with the pad of his finger.

She shivered and tightened her fingers in his hair as her world started to spin out of control. Within seconds, his fingers were slick with her juices and her hips rocked against his hand, guiding him to the places she craved him the most. He was a fast learner, and soon he had her panting, her legs trembling as pleasure bloomed inside her.

He shifted his big body into a new position, using his free hand to guide her right leg over his shoulder, opening herself to him completely.

"My *sadina*," he said, his voice possessive, the last syllables morphing into a growl that was more animal than man.

"Your dragon?"

"Is very pleased you and I are finally naked."

"Finally? We only met a few hours ago."

His eyes flashed and his voice changed, deeper and rougher than before. "Still too long."

His dragon had taken control for a moment. She knew it. Before she could confirm it, Karos' head was between her thighs. His tongue and fingers worked together, and every thought in her head vanished beneath a crashing wave of pleasure.

She could do nothing but ride the waves that rose and fell in time to the touch of his mouth. His tongue set tiny fires everywhere he touched her, and just as she thought she couldn't possibly take any more, he slid two fingers into her channel, filling her with hard, fast thrusts of his hand. He sucked the delicate pearl of her clit into his mouth and she came apart, uttering a broken, wordless cry as he continued his merciless onslaught, hurling her into an orgasm so strong she forgot to even breathe.

Her legs were still shaking when Karos rose to his feet, his hands landing on her waist as he moved in close and kissed her. She rose on her toes and kissed him back, rubbing herself against him, needing to feel his bare skin against hers. Their tongues tangled as they kissed. Hot, messy kisses punctuated by groans and whispers of each other's names.

"Need you," he said, his voice rough and raw.

"Need you, too."

He bent, cupping her ass in his hands and lifting her back into his arms. She loved that he could do that, his strength as sexy as everything else about this strange, amazing male. She twined her arms around his neck, fingers in his hair, mouth on his and wrapped her legs around his hips. The thick shaft of his cock pressed to the seam of her pussy, and she wriggled her hips, trying to bring them even closer together. She needed him inside her more than she needed her next breath.

He groaned into her mouth and lifted her higher, then lowered her so the broad head of his cock slowly slipped inside her. Her channel stretched around him, her body giving way to his until he was buried hilt deep inside her. They stayed that way for a moment. Not moving. Not speaking. Just…being. It was the most intimate thing she'd ever experienced.

When he raised his mouth from hers, she moaned in protest. She didn't want this to be over. Not yet. She wanted to stay connected to him in this one, brief moment of bliss.

"Do you feel it?" he asked, his tone hushed.

"I feel you. Us. For a second there it was perfect."

"Yes, it was, my *sadina.*"

He kissed her then. It started off slow and tender, but it quickly built to a crescendo as she kissed him back, and flexed her inner walls around his cock.

He groaned into her mouth and moved in a hard, steady rhythm, every stroke adding to the fire already burning inside her. She uttered a needy cry and met him thrust for thrust. His head fell back as passion overcame him, his movements growing harder and more erratic with every passing second.

His name fell from her lips again and again, until she realized her voice was echoing off the walls of the gym. She buried her face in the crook of his neck to muffle her cries as her reality unravelled, leaving her adrift in a realm of pure pleasure.

Her legs tightened around his hips as her orgasm neared and she rode his cock hard, taking everything he offered her and giving back in kind. At the moment of release, she closed her teeth on his skin, biting him as a scream tore from her throat.

He roared. A primal, wild cry that would have terrified her if anyone else had made it. His orgasm thundered through him and he pounded into her with bruising power. He bowed his head and bit her throat. Then, her senses exploded. For a moment she could feel Karos inside her, not just her body, but inside her soul. It didn't make sense and it was over far too quickly, but even afterward, she had a sense of connection with her lover that hadn't been there before.

When she finally came back to herself, Karos still held her, but his hold was gentler and he was nuzzling the side of her neck. "I am sorry. I did not mean to do that. But you bit me and I…I lost control."

She raised her head and smiled at him as he lifted his gaze to hers. "I didn't mean to bite you, either. Since I did it first, I think this one is on me."

"I shouldn't have done it."

"I'm taking it as a compliment. I made the big, bad dragon lose his mind for a second. I'll just have to wear a turtleneck tomorrow to hide the bruise, or we're going to have a lot of explaining to do."

He stroked a finger over the spot on her neck. "There is no mark. You will not need to hide anything from the others if you wish to do so."

She caught a note of discontent in his voice. "I don't know what I want to do about us, yet. This is all too new. Will you be in trouble or anything?"

He shook his head. "The Pyrosians understand that matings like ours happen without warning. They will be happy for us. I had already decided to inform Keth about it in the morning."

A flash of irritation hit. "Uh huh. When did you plan on mentioning it to *me*? I spent today wondering what the hell was wrong with me. I was in the middle of a crisis and couldn't stop thinking about you, when I should have been focusing on getting Hanna and Lily back."

Karos' expression turned sheepish. "I did not realize you were experiencing the *rux*. You are human, so I was not certain this even was a true mating fever at first. And while you might have felt unfocused, it did not show. Until that kiss, I had myself convinced that this would pass."

"You still should have told me."

"I haven't had to communicate my thoughts and

feelings to anyone since I left home. It will take me some time to remember how."

"Same here." She loosened her legs from around his hips as she spoke.

He took the hint, easing their bodies apart before setting her back on her feet and wrapping her in his arms again.

"We will learn this together. And when I frustrate you too much, we will come to this place and work through our frustration." He grinned. "I will have fond memories of this place now."

He wanted her to stay with him. In fact, he was talking like it was a given. She'd agreed to one night, not forever. She had a job to do. People to protect. She couldn't stay here. That was… She slammed the brakes on that entire train of thought. She could worry about that after they'd found Hanna and the others. This moment was just the calm before the storm, and she wanted to stay in it for as long as she could.

"I like this place too." She pointed at the ceiling. "But I think I'd like to add some fond memories of your place, too. Your bed has got to be more comfortable than the wall."

"It is." He kissed her tenderly, then released her. As she stepped away from him, he swept a hand between them, and in the space between heartbeats she found herself clad in a soft, sumptuous robe of deep crimson with a pair of soft slippers on her feet. He was dressed in an identical outfit, though his robe was trimmed in yellow.

"Thank you."

"It is my honour to gift you with anything your heart

desires, my *sadina*. All I have, and all I can create, is yours."

She followed him to the damaged door. "For now, all I want is a nice, soft bed, and another round of really incredible sex. Think you can handle that, Big Red?"

He gave her a look that made her blood sizzle in her veins. "I know I can."

———

CHAPTER SIX

———

Karos woke to an unfamiliar sensation – Megan was tracing gentle fingers over the scars that marked his back from shoulder to hip. He hadn't been with anyone since he'd been injured. The last beings to touch him had been the medical staff assessing his readiness to return to combat. Megan's caresses were far more pleasant.

"Good morning." He didn't move. Didn't want to do anything that would end the pleasure of having her hands on him. He had a confession to make to her this morning, and once he did, his mate would not be happy with him.

"Morning." Her voice was still husky with sleep. "How did you get these?" She stroked his back again.

"The war against the renegade temples. I was in dragon form at the time, and one of the enemy managed a lucky slash of her claws. She got my wing, too. I managed a controlled crash landing that saved my life, but it left me with those scars."

"Do they show in your dragon form, too?"

"They do. Though on my dragon they look different. The scales grew in white instead of red."

"And your wing?" She chuckled. "I can't believe I'm lying here asking you about your wings. It's hard to imagine you as anything as other than the man I see."

He rolled over to face her. "I will show you my dragon form soon. Then you will understand that I am not a man at all. I am Karos of the Romaki, your *sodono*."

She laid a hand on his chest, and he covered it with her own. Then, she sighed. "We still need to talk about that. I agreed to one night, and it was amazing, but forever? Like you said, we're not even the same species. I travel. You don't. We both have jobs. Plans. Lives. I'm not giving up everything to be your mate based on chemistry and your conviction that we're destined for each other."

He had to tell her. After last night, she wasn't human anymore, either. He'd bitten her, and he had broken the skin. His magic had flowed into her, binding their souls together. The bite had healed in seconds, and that could only mean one thing. She was Romaki now. It had happened before, with Prince Radek and his mate, Piper. He had no doubt it had happened again. But, how did he tell her that his loss of control meant she was already committed, and without her permission? Shame filled him. The Gods may have ordained their mating, but claiming her without permission was not honourable.

"I do not wish for you to give up anything, my *sadina*. We will both have to make adjustments." Even as he said it, he knew she'd be the one to face the greater share the changes, starting with the fact she was now Romaki, complete with a dragon spirit of her own.

"And yet, last night you were talking about me living

here, with you. That didn't sound like a compromise." She fixed him with a steady look, her jaw set and a hint of challenge in her eyes.

He started to answer but stopped and forced himself to consider his next words. It wasn't something he did often. He preferred to speak plainly. Tali had teased him about it for years, always warning him that when he found his mate, he'd have to change his ways. If she were here right now, she'd be laughing at him.

"I spoke without thinking," he admitted finally. "Merging two lives is something that all mated pairs must work through. Though I will confess, I never expected to be one of them. It is likely I will make mistakes." He paused, then added. "I made one last night."

Her lovely eyes widened and she pulled back from him.

"When I bit you, did you feel something? A moment of connection?"

She nodded, her expression still guarded. "Yeah."

"That was my mistake. I bit you. You didn't feel it, but I broke the skin and tasted your blood."

She stared at him. "But there wasn't any blood."

"Because you healed too quickly."

"Humans don't heal that fast." Her words were flat, her eyes wary. She understood, but she wanted him to confirm her suspicions.

"No, they don't. But Romaki do."

"What did you do to me?" Every word was carved in ice.

He grunted and raked his hand through his hair again. "I claimed you as my mate, Megan. Our souls were blended. I cannot regret that I did it, because you are mine, but I will forever regret that I did it without your permission."

"You mated me? That's what I felt last night?" Shock, anger, and something he couldn't name flashed across her face, and then her expression hardened.

He hung his head. "What you felt was the binding of our souls, yes. It is meant to be a special moment, the first of our lives together. I stole that from us. I am sorry."

"So am I. And I'm mad, too. You took away all my choices, Karos. I get that I didn't really have much, not the way this mating thing works with your species, but dammit! I deserve better than that." She frowned. "And you didn't tell me this last night. You waited. Again."

He stiffened and averted his eyes. "I know. I was selfish and weak. I should have had better control. I…" He swallowed, then uttered the words that seemed to define his life of late. "I failed you, and I was ashamed."

Her expression softened a little. "You definitely failed to communicate. I guess we're going to need to work on that. I don't think you need to feel ashamed, but you will definitely be making this up to me later." She sighed. "But we have other things to do first. Like get our friends back."

"Yes." He reached for her and drew her into his arms. She allowed it, and while she wasn't entirely relaxed, her next words had no edge to them.

"So, tell me the rest. I can heal faster, now. What else?"

"You are my mate in all ways."

"Lovely sentiment, but a little light on details. What exactly does that mean?"

He chose his next words carefully. "You are not only mated to a Romaki dragon, my beautiful *bakkia*, you are one."

"I'm a…" she stared at him, unable to finish the sentence.

"A dragon, with a dragon's spirit and magic."

"You turned me into a dragon? An actual, I have wings and a tail dragon?" her voice rose as everything finally came together. "And you didn't think that was an important tidbit to share? We really have to work on your communication. Mates or not, this will never work if you don't start telling me what's on your mind."

He winced, then gripped her flailing hands in his, and pulled her in tight to his body, his head bowed over hers. "I am sorry."

"You'd better be!" Her words came out with a low, rumbling growl that tore loose from her throat and rose, almost to a roar.

He hugged her, pressing his lips into her hair and holding her tight as she struggled to make sense of it all. "Softly, my *sadina*. Do not let your dragon seize control."

Megan uttered a frustrated snarl, but then she closed her eyes and slowed her breathing. After a moment, she relaxed a little, and her next words were entirely her own. "Tell me everything."

MEGAN'S SENSES spun and her thoughts whirled so fast she couldn't hold onto any of them. She had magic? And a dragon she needed to control? There wasn't enough coffee on the planet for this kind of morning.

"You are Romaki, now. Like Prince Radek's mate, Piper. Once human, now…not."

"I'm not human," she murmured, more to herself than

Karos. It was hard to grasp the idea. Especially while she was still feeling angry, hurt, and stunned by Karos' revelations.

"You are still yourself, Megan Richards. Your soul has not changed, but your body is Romaki now. Stronger. Faster. You will live for centuries, and you have a dragon spirit within you."

"One bite did all that?" She moved away from him a little. "This is not an auspicious start to our…whatever this is." She glowered at him. "You really should feel bad about this."

"I do."

The way his shoulders slumped and his head bowed made it clear that he felt like crap, which helped a little. Not a lot, but enough that when he reached for her again, she didn't pull away. It was probably the stupid *rux* making her feel this way, but she still craved his touch.

He held her for a few minutes in silence, and she nestled in his arms, working through everything she'd just learned. It didn't help much. She was still reeling, but time wasn't going to wait for her to get her head together. She'd have to suck it up and deal with everything later. "This isn't going to help us with our mission," she finally spoke up.

"You are right. But I want to do it anyway. We slept only a few hours. We have hours to go until the deadline. Keth and Eva would notify us if there was any news." He paused before adding. "And after what I told you, I wasn't sure you'd ever allow me to be this close to you again."

If she were in her right mind, she probably wouldn't. The *rux* was affecting her deeply, and if it made her act out of character, then it must be doing the same thing to him.

That thought helped her let go of a little more of her anger. He was as twisted up as she was. She was going to have to cut herself, and him, a little slack right now.

"I'm blaming the *rux* for all our current challenges. At least, the ones I can." She sighed, and her next words were tinged with doubt and more than a little frustration. "Do you think we'll get any news about our friends? I mean, we tried everything to locate Lily's transponder already, and nothing worked. It's not looking good." Which was yet another thing the *rux* was messing with. She should be desperately worried about Hanna and Lily, but she couldn't hold onto that feeling for long before it slipped away again.

"I believe that the Gods brought us together for a reason. And it wasn't so that we could begin our lives grieving for those we care about."

"I don't know your Gods. For that matter, I'm not overly familiar with the Creator my people believe in, but I want to believe you're right."

"Until I found you, I believed I was not worthy of Daga's notice. The Lady of Flame expects her followers to be honourable, brave, and strong. I have not always been so."

"Why would you think that? I haven't known you long, but you don't strike me as a coward, or a weak man." She tapped a finger to his chest and winked at him. "In fact, I know firsthand just how strong you are."

"The priests of my temple taught us that the Gods had many ways of showing their displeasure in us. Everything from illness to tragic misfortune was a divine message."

"And not having a mate was one of those messages?" she asked.

"So they told us."

She snorted in derision. "Let me guess. You could improve your status by supporting the temples more. Donations. Volunteering. Devoting time and energy to those who communed with this Lady of Flame."

"And Solun, Lord of Frost. It wasn't until the temples attempted to claim they were meant to rule in place of the leaders of the two clans that many of us realized the truth. By then, it was too late."

She nodded. "The same thing happens here. People lie, twisting beliefs and religions until it's not about faith anymore, it's all about power. Hanna's mission is to free the women and children caught up in such power plays and give them a safe place to start over."

"We will get them back. Her mission will continue."

She nodded and eased herself out of his arms. It was time to get back to work. "I'm going to need some clothes before I head back to my room. You made mine go poof, remember?" She waved to her naked body. "I have no idea how to handle this whole magic thing yet, so make with the mojo, please." She noticed how calm she felt and sighed. This *rux* thing was a pain. They'd just been talking about Hanna, and a few seconds later her worries had faded again.

He considered for a moment, then uttered a few words in his language and conjured an outfit for her.

Megan glanced down to assess what he had done. He'd conjured a pure black version of the uniform the embassy security staff all wore. It lacked the decorative touches and official heraldry of the real thing, but it was comfortable, as were the boots he'd created to go with it. "Perfect."

"I thought it might suit you."

"Can I wear this for the rest of the day? Or will it suddenly vanish at noon or something?"

"It will last as long as I draw breath, as will the footwear I conjured for you yesterday. I thought you might like to wear something that shows you belong here."

"You thought right." She gifted him with a soft, sincere smile. "Thank you." They still had a lot of talking to do, but she could still be gracious. After all, they were in this together, and it wasn't Karos' fault that his Gods were messing with them both.

MEGAN GOT TURNED AROUND MORE than once on her way back to her room, but she made it there eventually. The extra walking helped work some of the aches from her body, and a hot shower would fix the rest. It had been quite a while since she'd been involved with anyone, and even longer since she'd spent quality sack time with a lover as vigorous as Karos had proven to be.

Karos was a puzzle she was only beginning to piece together. He was a study in opposites. Compassionate but closed off. A loyal friend who seemed to spend most of his time alone. It was also clear to her that he felt responsible for everything, even things he couldn't control. And that was the easy stuff. He was also a freaking dragon. A magic-wielding, shapeshifting alien who had stolen her humanity from her... sort of.

She'd dismiss the whole idea as bat-shit crazy, but her standards for normal didn't apply at the moment.

She snorted in amusement. Her parents would be thrilled. They'd worried she'd never settle down. And as they grew older they worried less about grandbabies and more about who would be there for their daughter after they were gone. There were times she wondered about that, too, but she never let herself dwell on it for long. She'd manage, one way or another, just like she always had.

It wasn't until she took off the clothing Karos had conjured for her that she remembered the message scrawled across her legs. The memory of what had been done to her was followed by a rush of guilt and shame. She should have been looking for her friends, thinking about them. Holding them in her heart as she figured out a way to get them safely home. Instead, she'd fallen into bed with someone she barely knew. This *rux* thing was crazy-making in more ways than one.

By the time Megan left the shower, her fingers and toes were pruney. She'd scrubbed more of the markings off her legs, along with every trace of her misspent night with Karos. She *had* to focus.

When it came time to get dressed, she donned the clothes Karos had conjured. They were a perfect fit, and far better suited to her current needs than anything she'd packed. This was supposed to be a business trip. Her small carry-on suitcase was filled with clothing more appropriate to a boardroom than a brawl, and her only workout wear had been magicked out of existence last night.

She smiled at the memory of all the things they'd done once Karos had made their clothing vanish. Thinking of him elicited a pang of longing, as if they'd been separated for months instead of a matter of minutes. "This is ridiculous," she muttered and stomped back into the bathroom to finish getting ready. Try as she might, she couldn't shake the feeling.

Annoyed at herself, she leaned in close to the mirror, staring at her reflection. "Get it together. We have a job to do. We can get all mushy and moon-eyed over Karos after the job is done."

"*Karos.*" Someone whispered the word in a dreamy, decidedly feminine voice.

Her adrenaline spiked and she spun around, expecting to find someone standing behind her. "Who's there?" she demanded, looking around. No one was there.

"And now I'm hearing things. Great." She turned back to the mirror. "You can't afford to go crazy right now, Richards. How about we re-schedule this psychotic break for later, hmm?"

That's when it occurred to her - she wasn't hallucinating at all. "Dragon?" She said softly.

"*I am here,*" the same voice sounded in her head.

She froze. Holy shit. It was real, and it was talking to her.

"*Of course I am real.*" The voice sounded both amused and faintly reproachful.

The tiny part of her that kept denying what was happening finally gave up and flew a tiny white flag. This was happening.

"It's going to take me a bit to get used to all this."

"*I am a surprise. I understand. And you do not need to speak with voice. If you think at me, I will hear. We are one.*"

Her mouth opened, then she closed it again and thought back her response. "*You can hear this?*"

"*Yes.*"

She should have spent less time snuggling and more

time asking questions. There was too much she still didn't know.

"So, I can turn into a dragon now? Like Karos can?"

"Yes. We fly together. Fight together. We find friends. Save them. Protect them. Hurt ones who took them."

She liked the way her dragon thought. *"We will."*

"Soon?"

"I hope so."

Her head was still spinning as she donned the tactical webbing and weaponry she'd claimed from the armoury yesterday. She pushed her anger and shock aside and focused on what needed to happen next. She mentally rehearsed where each item was and how it worked, memorizing it so that if things got crazy, she wouldn't forget.

That was when her phone erupted into a strident whoop-whoop noise that sent her racing across the room to where it sat, recharging.

She unlocked the screen and opened the tracking app, then threw her hands in the air and cheered. "Yes, yes, yes! Way to go, Lily!" She raced out of the room, flying by bemused looking staffers as she pelted down the hall toward the elevator that led to the lower levels – and the command center. She knew where they were. Now, they just needed to figure out how to get them back.

<hr>

CHAPTER SEVEN

<hr>

MEGAN WAS in such a hurry she almost forgot to use the temporary access badge Karos had given her to activate the elevator. By the time she got the thing moving, her hands were shaking with excitement and the first rays of hope. It felt good, but she knew better than to give in to emotion. Any emotion. Hope was as dangerous as anger. Both led to bad decisions, and they were only going to get one shot at this. She needed to be thinking clearly. Karos would call the shots, but she was his partner. They'd figured this out together.

Keth was still in the command center, surrounded by several other Pyrosians as he barked orders in what she assumed was his native language. Maps of the city of Vancouver covered every monitor, and it only took her a few seconds to locate a pulsing orange beacon on the center screen, showing the same location as the app on her phone. He beckoned her to join them, a smile touching the corners of his mouth. He looked like he hadn't gotten much sleep, but then again, none of them had.

"You found them," he stated, relief and exhaustion in his voice. The others moved away, each returning to their assigned tasks, leaving the two of them alone.

"We found them," she replied. "Did you let Karos know? When I was in the armoury yesterday I forgot to ask about a radio. I had no way of letting him know, and I didn't want to miss anything, so I came straight here."

"Karos will be here momentarily." Keth's smile widened. "I believe he intended to stop by your room on the way to make sure you were aware of the situation."

"Oops."

Keth just fixed her with a mildly amused expression. "Given how close you two seem to be, I should probably assign you a room closer to his. It would save you both some walking."

Son of a bitch. He knew. Heat flooded her cheeks. Part of her wanted to duck her head and babble, but she ignored it. Denial wasn't going to do a damned bit of good. Karos had said that the others would be happy for them. It was time to see if he was right.

"Security cameras?" she asked in a conversational tone.

"Are everywhere," he confirmed. "And tend to get checked when someone melts the circuitry of one of the doors."

Crap. Talk about awkward. "Yeah. Sorry about the door. That wasn't my doing."

Keth nodded. "I'm aware. You won't have that kind of power for some time yet."

She blinked. "You know about that, too?"

"The camera captures images in..." he frowned. "I believe the term is high resolution," he said mildly.

"Then those cameras might end up capturing a murder when Karos gets here."

Keth laughed. "Please don't kill my head of security. I need him to get our people back."

The door opened and Keth's gaze moved from her to the new arrival. She knew without looking it was Karos. She could sense his presence. The energy in the room changed and something in her soul resonated to it.

"No murders," Keth murmured.

"I'm not making any promises." She looked around at the bustling room, then at the beacon flashing on the monitor. This wasn't the time or place for that conversation. Besides, Karos had been in the thrall of the *rux*. She knew he'd feel bad when he learned they'd been caught on film. He'd add it to the list of things he was already blaming himself for. Those broad shoulders of his must be carrying a hell of a lot of weight the way he kept adding to his burdens.

Karos strode over to them. She heard him coming but made an effort not to turn around despite an almost overwhelming desire to look his way. For a second, she thought she heard her dragon growling in frustration. *"We'll see him in a second. Cool your jets."*

"I am fire dragon, not wimpy ice dragon. I melt things, not cool them."

She bit back a giggle. Her dragon had an attitude, just like her.

Karos joined them a second later. He wore the same dark uniform as the other embassy guards, but he'd added a tactical harness festooned with enough weaponry to start a one-man war.

"Where are they being held?" he asked by way of

greeting, and then turned to smile down at her. "Hello, *sadina*."

"They are just outside one of the city's major ports. Small warehouse. Minimal foot and vehicle traffic in the area," Keth reported.

"Good. Minimal risk of bystanders becoming involved that way," Karos said.

"And no chance of getting close without being seen," Keth replied.

"We've got no chance of surprising them," Megan agreed. The Firsters had picked their location well, and she had no doubt it would be heavily defended.

Karos bared his fangs. "I have yet to meet a human who is not surprised when they spot a dragon headed their way."

Keth grinned fiercely. "Bring our companions home. I will alert the local authorities. They are aware we wish to handle this ourselves."

"I'm sure they're thrilled they're being excluded. How did you manage it?" Megan asked Keth.

"I called the Prime Minister. He'd rather this entire mess went away quickly and quietly. We're the ones best able to make that happen."

Karos chuckled. "You have been spending too much time with Jet."

Keth shrugged. "Diplomacy is not my preferred approach, but this time, it worked. I'll coordinate everything from here." He looked at Megan. "It's a good thing your device worked. The protesters we arrested yesterday have remained silent, and as you know, the government has a strict policy of never making deals with terrorists. As much as everyone wanted to safeguard the lives of those taken, no one was willing to release the prisoners."

She'd known that was a possibility, but she'd half-expected Keth and the Pyrosians to find a way around the rule. After all, this had the potential to set back alien/human relations for years – which was probably what the damned kidnappers were hoping for. "I'm glad, too. This way, we get to ruin those assholes' day. They think they've got us trapped between a rock and a hard place. Time for us to drop that rock on their heads." She smacked her left hand down on her right fist for emphasis.

Karos nodded, but he wouldn't meet her gaze. "I will end this."

"You mean we will. We. Plural. Because you agreed we were partners, Karos. We're doing this together, remember?

"I know what I agreed to, *sadina*. But the circumstances have changed since then."

"No, they haven't. My people are still in danger. It's my job, my responsibility, to get them out."

"You must stay here," he said.

Keth gave her an apologetic smile. "You need to speak with your mate about this, and there isn't much time." He pointed to a small door off one of the inner walls. You can use that room to speak privately. I'll continue to oversee things here."

He wanted them out of earshot for this conversation? That didn't bode well. She glanced at Karos, then nodded. "Lead the way."

Karos didn't say a word until the door slid shut behind them. It was a storage room holding extra chairs, and shelves containing a mixture of ordinary office supplies along with a few things she'd never seen before. Translucent cubes, thick items that looked like heavy pens of some kind, and an array of communication devices all lined up in what looked like charging docks.

"This better be good," she said.

Karos ran a hand through his hair, sending the red and silver strands into disarray. As unhappy as she was, she still had to fight the urge to walk over to him and smooth his hair back into place.

"I want you to know that this is not what I intended. I wanted you by my side today. I understand how important this is to you, " he said.

"And yet, you're telling me I can't be there, and I'm still waiting to hear a reason why."

"Because it's not safe."

She frowned. "I'm a professional bodyguard. It's my job to put myself into unsafe situations. That's pretty much my job description, in fact. And that was when I was human. Thanks to you, I'm a lot more than that."

"I know, but you still can't go."

"Why not?" she demanded, frustrated. "Is this some Romaki dragon macho thing? The little woman stays home while the man goes out to crack skulls and kick ass? Because that is not going to happen."

He actually smiled a little at that. And damn, it looked good on him. So good she wanted to—*Stay focused, dammit.*

"No, *sadina*. I will never ask you to stand down. Not once you have learned how to use your new abilities."

She caught on. "You bit me, and now you're telling me I can't go because I'm a *dragon*?"

"Your dragon's spirit will manifest soon. In the beginning, she will be undisciplined and difficult to control. If you go into battle with me now, before you have learned how to work with her, you could be hurt, or more likely, you will hurt someone else. Magic is driven by instinct and emotion, and you don't yet have the knowledge to use it safely. I have to protect you."

"No."

He blinked. "What?"

"I said no. No, you don't have to protect me. My job is to protect others. It's not just a job, either, it's who I am. You can't take that away from me."

"You are a danger to yourself and others right now, which means you aren't coming. I've already left instructions that you are to be kept here, under guard. If you try to leave the embassy, you will be stopped. I will not fail to protect someone else I care about. I cannot go through that again."

"Again? Is this about your friend?" She was angry, but not so much that she didn't hear the undertone of grief and pain in his voice. She didn't want to be a source of pain for him.

"I lost every friend I had during the war. Most of them in a single day." He exhaled sharply and his eyes clouded over. "The day after I was wounded, my friends decided to avenge me. They formed a raiding party and went after the ones who had injured me. They did it without authority, and no one knew where they had gone until it was too late. They were discovered by a much larger force. None of them returned."

This was making more sense by the minute. "Was one of them called Tali?"

It took him a few seconds to answer. "How do you know that name?"

"You called out to her in your sleep. You were having a nightmare, I think. You kept calling her name and asking her to forgive you. I thought maybe she was a lover, someone who left you."

He shook his head. "Not my lover. My best friend. The one I trusted to guard my back. I failed her. Wasn't there when she needed me most."

She cocked her head to one side and fixed him with a questioning stare as the pieces started to fall into place. "How did you fail her, exactly?"

"I told you. I wasn't there for her. They all died because of me."

"That's bullshit. They died because they did something foolish and got caught."

He stiffened and took a step back from her, his head shaking in denial. "That's not what happened."

"You're the one who told me the story. What did I get wrong?" She folded her arms across her chest and watched as he started to pace, his gestures agitated.

"I should have been there. We made a pledge to watch out for each other. To guard each other's lives with our own."

"That doesn't make any sense," Megan said.

He looked at her in confusion. "It makes sense to me."

"Clearly. But whatever happened to your friends, it's not going to happen to me. I need to be there today." She let him hear her frustration and anger, but it didn't make any difference.

He shook his head. "It's too great a risk. You are mine to protect. Later, I will teach you all you need to know, and together we will protect everyone we care about. Today, please trust me to do what you cannot."

"You mean what you won't let me do." She threw her hands in the air in frustration. "I can do this."

"I am sorry." He reached for her again, but she stepped out of reach.

"Stop apologizing and start listening to me! Teach me what I need to know and let me come with you." She already knew he wasn't going to relent. He was afraid he'd lose her the way he'd lost Tali and the others.

"I am listening. I hear you, but I can't allow it. When this is over, I will take you to my bower and talk to you about anything you wish. Teach you all you need to know. And make love to you until we are both exhausted. I will make you a home fit for a queen and fill it with every comfort I can imagine. This is how it should be amongst my race. I have been a poor mate to you." He sighed, and some of the light went out of his eyes. "I don't deserve to have you as my mate."

"Your Gods seem to think otherwise." And if she was honest with herself, so did she. He was overprotective and bossy, sure, but he was also honourable, noble, and *hers*.

KAROS WAITED for her to say something more, but his beautiful mate had lapsed into silence, her arguments at an end. It didn't give him the peace of mind he'd hoped for. All it did was add to his doubts. He'd taken this choice from her when he'd claimed her. Could she forgive him for that?

Squaring his shoulders, he met her gaze and offered her the only solace he could. "I will bring our friends home safely. I swear it."

Her eyes still shadowed by frustration and hurt, she mustered a bittersweet smile and nodded. "You'd better."

He understood how difficult this was for her. A warrior's place was in battle, but her abilities were too new. Too much could go wrong. He'd lost everyone he cared about once already. He couldn't go through that again. He pressed his hand to his heart. "I will not fail."

He wanted nothing more than to take her into his arms and kiss her until her smile returned, but there wasn't time. His heart tore open as he turned away, denying himself another taste of her sweet lips. He was needed elsewhere, and she had to remain here, where she was safe. He was partway out the door when she spoke again. "And you better come back in one piece, too. I'm not done being mad at you, yet."

He walked back into the command center feeling like he'd failed – again. This time he'd do what he couldn't the last time, though. This time, he'd protect everyone.

"*She is angry,*" his dragon commented.

"*But I am right. We must protect our mate.*"

The beast within was silent for a long moment before it finally replied. "*She is our mate. We protect.*"

Having Megan with them was too great a risk, both for her, and for everyone around her.

Keth shot him a look and joined him as he walked toward the door. "I feel like I should be offering congratulations on your mating, but given the situation…" He trailed off. "How displeased is she?"

"Very," Karos said tersely. "And she has good reason."

"More than one. You forgot about the security cameras in the gym, my friend. I've wiped the footage and ensured no one else saw it, but I had to tell her."

"Daga's flaming wrath, I never thought about that." Another wave of shame and anger washed over him.

"It's been dealt with." Keth waved open the door and continued to walk with him. "How is she taking the news?"

Karos snorted. "About as well as you would expect. She is angry. Frustrated with me. And her dragon's spirit is already stirring. Which will only amplify all that she is feeling. It is a good thing she does not know how to breathe fire yet, or I would be scorched." The presence of her dragon would also ramp up his mate's mating fever. It had only been a few hours since he'd last taken her, and the need to have her again was a fire in his blood. He couldn't be away from her for long, or his beast would rebel, as would hers.

"How long do you have before the *rux* takes hold again?" Keth asked softly.

"Long enough. But not by much. We will need to go into the mountains before midday. We will not return until the *rux* fades."

"I know how it is. We'll see to things here and explain matters to Megan's friends." Keth grinned. "Just remember to take a communicator with you so we can keep in touch."

"I will do so. But now, I need to go. My mate needs to stay here, where it's safe."

Keth met his gaze. "I will have Eva stay with her."

"Thank you, my friend."

Keth surprised him by asking, "Do you truly believe this is the right choice? Leaving her behind?"

He answered without hesitation. "I do."

His dragon rumbled, his displeasure clear. The beast didn't want to be separated from his mate.

"And your other half?" Keth asked.

"Is of a differing opinion."

"I thought he might be."

He shot the other male an inquiring look. "Why?"

"Because we are stronger when we stand with our mates. They make us better than we were. Eva is a gift from the Gods, one I am thankful for every day." Keth raised his hands. "In this case, I agree with your dragon. But it's your decision, not mine."

"She stays here." There was no other option. He couldn't risk her life. He would not repeat the mistakes of his past. He wouldn't survive that kind of loss again.

Keth nodded once and stopped walking. "Then I will wish you good hunting and return to the command center. The transports will be leaving soon."

"Our friends will be with us again soon."

'And the ones who took them?"

Karos bared his fangs. "Will learn what happens when you mess in the affairs of dragons."

Keth threw back his head, laughed, and waved him on his way.

Karos made for the upper levels. It was time to put an end to this threat, once and for all. Once that was done, he could be alone with Megan and show her what it meant to be mated to a dragon.

CHAPTER EIGHT

MEGAN HAD to wait until everyone's attention was elsewhere before she slipped out of the command center. Keth had stuck close to her since seeing Karos off, and she got the impression he was keeping an eye on her. Probably to make sure she didn't do exactly what she was planning on doing.

She'd spent the intervening time gathering information on the area her friends were being held, working out approach routes, travel times, and trying to make her best guess as to what kind of defences she might find when she got there. Now, she just needed to figure out how to make that happen.

"*We fly,*" her dragon suggested.

"*I don't even know how to become a dragon. Magic isn't something we humans understand.*"

Her dragon stirred and rumbled, sounding amused. "*Not human now. Have me.*"

"*I do. But that doesn't mean I know what to do with you. You didn't come with an instruction manual.*"

She paced the length of the room again, then glanced around. Keth was conversing with several other Pyrosians and he'd turned his back to her. It was time to go. Karos needed to learn something very important about his mate. She didn't take orders very well.

"Mate is wrong. We go. We save. We fight together." Her dragon sounded as annoyed as she was.

"He is wrong. This isn't his fight. It's ours."

There was a rush of approval from her dragon, but that didn't quiet the worry that welled up inside her. If she disobeyed her mate and put herself in this fight, he wouldn't react well. Not with the guilt and grief he carried.

She understood that kind of guilt. She'd experienced it herself more than once. Karos had lost friends, and there was a truckload of guilt tangled up with his grief. If they were going to make this work, he had to accept that he couldn't protect her from every threat. Her mother had always told her it was always best to begin as you intend to continue, and that meant she needed to be there today. She wasn't going to be left behind. Not now. Not ever. Karos would have to accept that about her. She closed her eyes and whispered a soft prayer to her ancestors. "Please, help him understand."

She exited the command center casually, resisting the urge to slink or tiptoe out. Karos hadn't said anything about restricting her movements inside the embassy, only that she wasn't to leave the compound. No sense tipping anyone off to her plans until she had to.

She walked briskly along the empty corridor toward the elevator, her head full of potential plans. She was armed and ready. Now, she just needed to find a way out of the embassy without being seen.

Even if she could figure out how to turn into a dragon, she had no idea how to navigate from the air, and she was pretty sure Google maps didn't have a dragon-flight mode.

When the elevator doors opened on the main level, Eva was standing there, her smile as sunny as a summer day. "Going somewhere?"

Dammit. "If I say yes, are you going to try and stop me?"

"Nope." The blonde woman's smile widened. "I'm here to aid and abet your escape."

Megan blinked in surprise. "You are?"

"You bet I am. You are now a member of the "Mated to an alien" sisterhood. I'd give you the welcome speech, but we're on a deadline and I can give you the basics while we drive."

"Sisterhood, huh? I like the sound of that. Do we get a secret handshake?"

Eva laughed and pointed down the hall. "We're going this way. And no, there's no handshake. No manual, either. Just moral support, advice, and a sympathetic ear when your mate invariably does something that makes you want to toss him out an airlock."

"You mean like forgetting to mention that they mated you and you're not human anymore?" Megan asked.

Eva winced. "That would definitely count. They try their best, but there are times…" she shook her head. "They might look human, but our males are from very different worlds. The Pyrosians have so few females left on their planet they are insanely protective of their mates. Keth wouldn't let me out of his sight for the first few weeks we were mated. It's taken time for him to adjust to the idea that he can't wrap me in cotton batting and lock me away for the rest of our lives."

"He's going to lose his mind when he finds out you're helping me, isn't he?"

Eva laughed and shook her head. "He knows where I am, and he told your mate that I'd be with you. He just didn't say where *you'd* be."

"Your mate is sneaky. Tell him thanks the next time you see him."

Eva smiled and tapped her temple. "I just did."

"Telepathy?"

"Mmhmm. Romaki mates aren't the only ones who get some interesting abilities."

This day kept getting stranger, and she still hadn't had a single sip of coffee to help her cope. "So, how are we getting out of here?" Megan asked as they walked.

"Keth's arranged for a car, and I've got clearance to leave the embassy. Keth sent all the information we'll need to catch up with Karos and the others to my phone already."

That information stunned her to silence for a second. "Why?" she finally asked.

"Because Keth has learned the lessons your mate hasn't yet. Mated pairs are stronger when they are together. He tried to tell Karos, but he wasn't ready to hear it. You need to be there, for your friends, and for him." She turned to Megan and shrugged. "Besides, short of a nuclear weapon or flying directly into a star, the only thing that can hurt a Romaki dragon is another dragon. Since you and Karos are the only ones around, you're pretty much invincible. There's no reason you shouldn't be there."

Megan's mouth fell open. "Say that again?"

"You're an armour-plated, fire-breathing badass."

She was going to roast Karos' chestnuts when she saw him again. "My mate failed to mention that to me. He said I could be a danger to myself and others."

Eva shook her head. "The war cost him everyone he cared about. He doesn't talk about it much, but Vykor filled in a few details and Keth got more information from Prince Radek. Karos lost so much. He's trying to protect you…and himself."

"He's also a lousy communicator."

Eva snorted. "They all seem to have that in common. Welcome to the sisterhood."

"Thank you." Megan was still trying to wrap her head around the revelation that not only was she a dragon now, she was also a force of nature. No one would be able to threaten her friends again.

They ducked in and out of dimly lit maintenance tunnels for what felt like forever, but eventually, they reached a massive parking garage full of vehicles. Some were clearly civilian, others were identical to the limo she'd ridden in yesterday. There were several large, empty spaces down the far end, which she guessed must have held the transports Karos and others were using.

"This one." Eva pointed to a dark red sports car that looked like it cost more than Megan's annual salary. The windows were heavily darkened, and she knew once they were inside, no one would see her.

"That must be Jet's." Megan hadn't known the

Pyrosian diplomat long, but the car looked like it would be to his taste. Expensive, elegant, and built for speed.

Eva snickered. "Yeah, it's his. All part of his playboy alien image."

"Image?" Megan dropped into the passenger seat.

"Don't tell him I said this, but yeah, it's all an image. He's actually a really sweet guy. He's the eldest son of an old, very noble house on Pyros. Lesser royalty, with all the headaches and expectations that come with that kind of life. His family is big on appearances, but it's mostly an act for him. I know you're worried about your friends, but Jet will do anything he can to keep Hanna and Lily safe." Eva started the engine and headed out.

They didn't have to so much as slow down on their way out of the embassy. All she had to do was stay out of sight until they were beyond the gates. Once they were clear, Eva gave her a thumbs up signal and she scrambled back into her seat and strapped in.

The sky was brightening slowly, heralding the coming dawn as they flew along the streets of Vancouver at speeds that made the rest of the traffic look like they were still in park.

She picked up the thread of their earlier conversation. "It helps to know my friends have someone competent and kind with them." She wasn't going to stop worrying until everyone was freed and safe, but Eva's words helped settle the worst of her worries for now.

"Vykor is a good male, too. Quiet, but determined to do the right thing."

"But he doesn't have a dragon."

"And he survived on Romak without one. Which makes him the bravest, strongest male I've ever met."

"That bad?" she asked.

"I met Keth the day of the bombing. In fact, he saved my life. We travelled back to Pyros with Prince Radek and his mate, Piper. I learned all about the problems on Romak. As much as we tend to think that the more technologically-advanced species have things all figured out, no world is perfect."

"I guess not," Megan said. She'd known about the problems with the temples, the fear-mongering, and finally, the war on Romak, but she hadn't considered what it all must have been like for someone like Vykor. Someone different. Someone others feared.

They rode in silence for a few minutes before Megan said, "We're going to get them back. All of them."

"Of course we are. These Humanity First idiots are driven by fear." Eva's hands tightened on the steering wheel. "We're going to show them why they should really be afraid of us. Not because we're taking human women, or influencing humanity's evolution, but because we can kick serious ass when we're threatened."

Megan glanced over at the petite blonde with the bubbly personality and sweet smile. "We are?" she stressed the first word.

Eva nodded, her golden eyes burning with an inner fire that made them look like molten gold. "We are. I'm not human either, Megan. I'm a mated Pyrosian, and I throw a mean fireball."

Whoa. "Fireballs? You?"

Eva held out her right hand, palm up, and snapped her fingers. A split second later her hand was enveloped in flames. They vanished a moment later, and she set her hand back on the steering wheel. "I am small but mighty."

She said with a soft laugh. "But since I'm not bulletproof, I'll be staying behind you."

"I'm bulletproof?"

Eva nodded. "In dragon form, yeah. You ever play Dungeons and Dragons?"

"I had a boyfriend who talked me into playing for a while, yeah. Why?"

"Because you're about to join the real thing. I'm a spellcaster, and you, my dear, are a tank. One with wings, scales, and a breath weapon that can level buildings."

Megan thought about that for a second. "I think I'm good with that."

"I thought you might be." Eva checked the map again. "We'll be there soon. You ready to ruin the bad guys' day?"

"You know it."

Eva reached for the stereo and pushed the play button. Wagner's Flight of the Valkyries filled the car.

It was perfect.

KAROS FINISHED COORDINATING HIS TEAMS, making sure they were all in position. They were doing a final comms check when a new sound reached his ears: the roar of a car engine and a compelling crescendo of music. What in the name of Solun's hoary beard was it, and how had it gotten past his established checkpoint?

The answer came when the doors opened, and two females who had no business being there stepped into the grey morning light. Eva was wearing one of the Pyrosian security uniforms, which doubled as body armour, custom-fitted to her small stature. Keth had it made for her in case the embassy was ever attacked. This was not an attack, though, and she should be back at the embassy, out of harm's way.

Megan walked with a determined stride toward them, still wearing the tactical vest and weaponry he'd loaned her. Her face was set in a stubborn mask, and her dark eyes glittered with a dangerous light as she closed the distance between them.

He went out to meet her. "You are both supposed to be back at the embassy."

"I'm supposed to be here, getting my friends back." Megan's voice held a hint of a growl he found arousing despite her blatant defiance.

"Keth was supposed to—"

Eva cleared her throat. "My mate told you that I would stay with Megan. He never said anything about where we'd be at the time."

Karos ground his teeth together. "I need to protect my mate. Megan, we talked about this."

Megan met his gaze squarely. "And I need to be here, doing what I can to save my friends." She smiled a little. "Alongside my mate.""

Eva spoke again. "You know as well as I do that a Romaki dragon doesn't need anyone's protection, Karos."

"Which is something else you forgot to mention," Megan added, her dark eyes narrowing, and for the first time, he saw a gleam of gold in their depths. Her dragon was making its presence known in every way it could.

"You shouldn't be here, *sadina*. You aren't ready for this." Even as he said the words, he knew they weren't true. It was what he'd told himself because it was easier than dealing with the fear of losing someone else he cared about.

"If I'm not ready, then I better get there fast, because you're not going in there without me. Tell me what to do, dammit. I'm not sitting this one out." She stepped up to him and laid a hand on his chest. Her voice softened. "Karos, please. You told me that your Gods chose me to be your mate. If this is what's meant to be, then why won't you let it happen? You promised me we were partners."

"We are." He covered her hand with his. "But I can't lose you."

"Then teach me how to protect myself. According to Eva, you're a fire-breathing badass. Show me how to be one, too. I trust you to protect me. Will you trust me to watch your back, the way you trusted Tali?

His fear burned away in a rush of fierce pride and desire. This was his mate. His everything. And he couldn't deny her anything, not even this. He trusted her with everything he was – including his life. "I trust you."

She started to argue again, then grinned up at him as she registered what he'd said. "Say that again."

"I trust you with my heart, my soul, and my life, Megan Richards. We will do this together, despite the risks. The Gods are crazy, and so are you."

He pulled her into his arms and kissed her, drinking in her courage and beauty until he was drunk on it. Their tongues danced, bodies melting into each other. His fingers stroked through the warm weight of her hair, and she slipped her arms around his waist and pulled herself in tight against him. Gods, she was incredible. He didn't deserve her, but he finally understood that it didn't matter. She was his. He'd have to find a way to be worthy of her.

When he finally raised his head, she grinned up at him, her eyes dancing now. "Now what?"

He looked around, trying to estimate how much room they would need for what came next. "Now, we free our friends. Eva, you may want to give us some room. And tell the others we'll be moving on the target soon."

Eva nodded. "What's the go signal?"

"Two dragons taking to the sky," he replied.

"Gotcha." Eva beamed at them both, then moved to where the others were waiting.

"So, what do I do?" Megan asked.

"Find your calm. Center yourself. You need to be the one in control at all times, though she will need to be part of everything you do. It is a difficult balance to maintain. Our dragons are our instincts, the wild, dark part of our natures. If you let her take over too much, especially so soon, there's no telling how much damage she might do."

"Calm. Right. Anything else?"

"When you're ready, speak to your beast. Call her forward, invite her to manifest. She will control the change. Once that happens, follow my lead. Whatever you think, your dragon will do, so long as you stay calm and focused."

"Even breathe fire?"

"Definitely that. Choose your targets carefully, though. I will transform first, and that way we'll be able to speak mind to mind once you have done so."

Her eyes widened. "Telepathy?"

"Dragons can't speak. Mind to mind is the only way to communicate while we're transformed."

Megan nodded. "I think I've got it. Stay focused. Stay

in control. Telepathy to talk. Oh, can I use my guns while I'm uh…shifted?"

"No. They will transform with you. Later, I'll teach you how to conjure clothing. For now, remember to think of yourself dressed when you return to this form."

"Or what happens?"

"You'll reappear naked, and then I'll have to kill any male who sees you."

"Possessive much?"

He bared his fangs at her. "Very. And while I'm affected by the *rux*, it won't be something I can prevent. I'm riding the edge of my control as it is. Once our friends are free, we need to leave."

"We do?"

"We'll have time to be sure they're alright. That's all. The *rux* grows stronger every second, and the longer we stay, the greater the risk the dragons take control. No one wants that. A dragon in *rux* is uh… hard on buildings."

"I can imagine."

She stood on her tiptoes and brushed a kiss to the corner of his mouth. "Show me what you look like as a dragon, my *sodono*."

It was the first time she'd spoken the word, and his heart thundered with pleasure as he kissed her once more, then walked into the middle of the street. Without a word, he turned to face her and summoned his dragon. It was time to teach these fools who and what they were dealing with.

MEGAN HADN'T BEEN sure how Karos would react to her

arrival. She'd known it wouldn't be easy for him, and she'd been prepared for him to be angry with her, pushing her away or even trying to order her to leave. She knew what it cost him to let her stay, and it humbled her that he'd paid that price, and more besides.

He'd fought his demons for her. She'd seen it happen, the shadows that had chased through his eyes, the way he'd clenched his jaw and flexed his hands as if preparing himself for an attack. Only the attackers had been inside his own head, the voices of doubt, grief, and guilt that had plagued him since the death of his friends.

She'd wanted to go to him. Touch him. Soothe his pain, but she knew better. He'd had to face this fight alone, but it was the last one. From here on in, they'd always fight together. She knew it in her heart, which raced with joy at the thought. There were other feelings, too. Something that felt like the beginnings of love. It was too soon for it to be real, but she already sensed that in time, love could come. In fact, she was certain of it.

She held onto that joy and anticipation as he kissed her and walked away, a low growl of sexual frustration leaving her lips as the distance between them grew. He'd been right about the *rux*. It was getting hard to ignore. Her blood was on fire, and her thoughts were full of sexual fantasies that all featured a tall, redheaded warrior whose touch she craved with every breath.

She wasn't sure what to expect when he transformed, and when it happened, she almost missed it. One second her lover stood there, arms at his sides and his eyes on her. The next, he was replaced by a massive creature covered in deep crimson scales that shimmered in the grey morning light. His head was the size of a car, and she took an involuntary step backward as he raised his head and stretched out his wings, putting himself on display for her.

"Holy shit," she breathed.

Karos walked over to her, his footfalls shaking the ground as he moved. His tail swung behind him, lashing slowly from side to side like a contented cat. When he reached her side, he lowered his head, so she was staring into one beautiful golden eye. Despite the changes, his eyes were the same. This was Karos.

He rumbled deep in his throat and she could feel it vibrate the ground beneath her feet.

"Later, I'm going to want to get a better look at you, but I guess we don't really have for that right now, do we?"

He nudged her gently, though even his lightest touch was almost enough to knock her off balance. Then he moved away from her, giving her space.

She watched him go, and when he stopped and swung back to look at her, she knew it was time. She kept her gaze locked on him, took a deep breath, and spoke to the beast she could feel pacing within the confines of her mind. *Show me what you've got, girl.*

She'd forgotten to ask if it would hurt, and she tensed with sudden worry as a strange, liquid sensation flowed through her. It was like her entire body had turned to water and was being poured into an unfamiliar container, giving her a new shape.

Never hurt you. We are one. Her dragon's voice was full of smug satisfaction and the same liquid shift happened inside her mind as the dragon's spirit took control, leaving her a passenger in her own body. It was a weird feeling, but it passed quickly, and when she regained control, the world looked different.

For one thing, she was a hell of a lot taller. Her senses seemed sharper, too. She could smell the concrete, still damp from last night's rain. She could also smell the Pyrosians, and the subtle differences between their scent and Eva's. Information poured into her-- scents, sounds, colours, and even flavours. She could taste the chemical residue of the fuel their vehicles had burned, the rich salt tang of the sea air, and beneath it all, she caught a hint of something familiar. Something important. Hanna.

She swung her head around and nearly careened into Karos, who had appeared at her side while she'd been getting her bearings.

"Slow, easy movements. This body is far larger and more powerful than the one you are used to." Karos' voice, as steady and strong as always, sounded inside her head.

"You can say that again. What do I look like? Do I look like you?" she thought back to him.

"You are as beautiful as a sunrise. Red, gold, and breathtaking."

She resisted the urge to preen and tried to focus on getting used to her new form. She flapped her wings a few times, raising her head on her long, sinuous neck to look down at the others. They looked much smaller now, and Eva was grinning like a lunatic.

"Looking good!" the little blonde called to her.

"Okay, I think I've got the basics. Now what?" She thought to Karos.

"We fly."

Okay. Fly. Sure. She watched as he moved away and launched himself into the air with strong, steady beats of his wings. The downdraft swirled around her, and it was like standing under a helicopter as it lifted off.

What the hell am I doing? She asked herself.

"We fly. We fight. We win." Her dragon sounded downright gleeful as it took over control long enough to send her soaring into the air after Karos. The creature didn't stay in control for long, but she was in the forefront of Megan's mind, making small corrections and helping her manage her new body.

She dipped her head to look back at the others, peering under one of her wings in a move that would have been impossible in her human form. Eva and the others had broken into teams, and they were on the move.

"Plan?" she asked Karos.

"We're the distraction. We're going to light up the sky with fire, but don't hit anything with it. We want everyone inside to come running out. The Pyrosians will pick them off."

That didn't sound terribly heroic, but then again, they had no idea where in the building Hanna and the others were being held. They could tear open the building or set it on fire, but they'd risk injuring the ones they'd come here to save.

"How?" she asked.

"Visualize. Focus."

"Fire! Burn!" her dragon sounded like a child on Christmas morning, and she had to take a moment to tighten her control on the creature. She clamped down too hard as one of her wings fell out of rhythm, throwing her off balance, and she yawed to one side. She squawked in alarm and backed off again, and her dragon took over, steadying her flight.

"Oops." She wasn't sure if the thought was hers or her

dragon's, though she could feel the creature's consternation.

Karos swung his head around, his golden eyes dark with concern.

"I'm okay. Just a brief miscalculation."

"Miscalculations can be painful. You might be hard to kill, but we feel pain like every other being." His voice was gentle, but she could hear the worry in his words, as well as the memory of his own remembered pain.

"I'll be careful."

His only response was to utter a snort of disbelief and the open his jaws in a grin that showed a mouthful of dagger-sharp teeth before flying off toward their target.

She fell in behind him, gaining confidence with each stroke of her wings.

"Follow me." Karos angled his wings and dropped into a dive, roaring loudly enough to rattle the windows of nearby buildings as he flew.

She followed moments later, full of exhilaration as the wind howled and she raised her voice in a roar of challenge and joy. As he passed over the top of the building that housed their friends, Karos loosed a jet of flame that seared the air and lit up the area in a blaze of light.

She copied him, trusting her dragon to do what was needed. All she did was visualize what she wanted, and it happened, though not as elegantly or impressively as Karos had done.

"Our mate is strong. We will learn. Be like him."

"Yes, we will." Her hearing was acute enough she could hear the cries of alarm coming from inside the building,

accompanied by panicked voices and the squawk of radios.

They swung around for another pass, and as she dropped into her next dive, the first wave of enemies fled the building and were met by a steady barrage of weapons fire from the Pyrosian forces. It was like no other firefight she'd ever witnessed. The aliens fought with energy weapons that made next to no noise, so the only sound came from the unsteady rounds fired back by the enemy.

The battle below distracted her, and her next bout of flame struck the corner of a nearby warehouse. *"Oops."*

"Oops again?" Karos sent.

"You can say you told me so later, Big Red. How do I put out that fire?"

"You don't. Eva will. I believe Keth sent her along for this reason. Her abilities to manipulate fire are impressive."

Eva. She'd forgotten about her in all the chaos. She rose into the air again and looked around until she spotted her. The little blonde was standing at the back of the embassy's strike teams. She was gesturing with her hands, and it took Megan a moment to realize that the little blonde was summoning balls of fire about the size of a soccer ball and lobbing them into the enemy ranks, creating chaos and carnage with every toss. Karos roared and Eva looked up. When she spotted the fire, she threw out a hand, and Megan watched in amazement as the little blonde drew the fire into her, gathered it between her hands, and tossed it at a group of reinforcements that spilled out the door of the building in a disorganized surge.

"Protect!"

The single word tore through her mind with stunning force as the unmistakable roar of a dragon filled the air.

Men screamed, and there was a sound of gunfire, panicked and sporadic from somewhere inside.

"What the hell was that?"

"Not what. Who," Karos thought to her. *"Vykor. Welcome to the skies. What happened?"*

There was no answer, at least none she could hear, but a few seconds later there was a thunderous noise and one corner of the building buckled outward and gave way. Metal screeched, masonry crumbled, and a massive form stepped through the hole.

Vykor was the colour of storm clouds, dark blues and purples that were both lovely and foreboding. Behind him walked two figures, their arms wrapped around each other's waists as they helped each other through the debris left in the wake of Vykor's self-made exit. Hanna and Jet. Relief filled her, but she kept looking, trying to catch sight of Lily.

She caught her scent first. Lily was bleeding. Badly. She roared in denial and dove, desperate to get to the ground and her friends.

"Slowly. Landing isn't easy." Karos murmured, his words a gentle whisper in her mind.

"I have to find Lily! She's hurt, and I can't see her."

"Look again. Vykor carries her on his back."

She eased back on her dive and took another look. There. Karos was right. Lily lay across the new dragon's back, not moving, her face pressed to his scales. She could still smell her blood, though, blended with the acrid scent of fear, fire, and gun smoke.

Worry for her friends overrode everything else, and she raced for the ground.

"Megan, slow down!" Karos barked the order, and she

belatedly realized she had no idea how to land. She'd been so focused on returning to the ground that she had pushed her dragon to the back of the mind, and as the ground rose to meet her, she stretched out her wings and allowed her other half to take control.

It was too late.

She hit the ground hard, talons carving gouges in the concrete and her wings flapping furiously. Her momentum carried her across the open space in a blink of an eye, and she could only watch in resignation as she hurtled out of control, straight into the steel wall of the neighbouring warehouse.

Everything went dark for a second, her senses to scrambled to make any sense, though she didn't think she was badly injured. At least, she didn't feel more than slightly shaken, and mortified at her inept attempt to land.

"*Are you alright? And do not even think about saying oops again,*" Karos sent to her.

"*How about ow?*" She shook her head, trying to clear it and get to her feet at the same time. She wasn't one hundred percent successful at either goal, but she did manage to untangle herself from the wreckage of what had been a wall and stagger back a few steps.

Karos appeared at her side, one of his wings extending over her back, his head level with hers. "*Are you hurt?*"

"*Just my pride, I think. I'm starting to see why you didn't want me along for this adventure.*"

He snorted, the sound echoing off the nearby buildings. "*And I am starting to realize I should have never tried to keep you away.*"

"*Partners?*"

"*Yesterday we were partners. Today, we are mates.*"

There was an underlying tone of possessiveness and contentment to his words that she wanted to savour, but there were other things they needed to be doing now. Friends they needed to check on. An enemy to be vanquished. She listened for a moment, noting the lack of gunfire.

Hanna called out. "Oi, Romaki dragonmen, Lily needs help over here."

Right. Hanna had no idea Megan was a dragon now. Nor did anyone else in their group.

"I need to change back," she told Karos.

"Visualize your other body, and don't forget your clothes."

"Clothes and guns. Got it." She did what he said, and after another disorienting shift of perceptions and that strange, liquid feeling, she was back on two legs again. And dressed.

Phew.

Karos had already finished the change by the time she got herself together, and they raced toward the others.

As she ran, she heard Hanna's normally calm voice break into a squawk of surprise. "Megan. That was you? What the hell is going on, and why can you turn into a dragon?"

CHAPTER NINE

KAROS STOOD with Megan as the embassy's medical staff assessed and treated their injured. A medical team had accompanied them but stayed out of range of the fighting until hostilities had ended. Law enforcement was now on the scene, and several media vehicles were already on site.

He wanted to take Megan and be gone from this place, and it was taking all his will to resist the demands of his body and wait for news about Lily.

The *rux* was making it hard for him to think clearly, and he was too agitated to stay still, so he paced. Megan walked with him, her lush mouth pressed into a tight line, and her fingers flexing in time to her steps. She was feeling the same need he was, and she had less than a day's experience with her new condition. Over time, the dragon's spirit could be tempered, but in the beginning it could be overwhelming. He had to get her away from here, soon. For both their sakes.

Jet and Hanna were being treated for minor injuries, and several Pyrosian officers were having their wounds healed. All the Pyrosians would make a full recovery, which was more than could be said for the enemy. The anti-alien movement was shattered; what was left of their leadership had been killed or captured, including the male behind the abduction. He still had questions about Lily's possible involvement , but he would have to wait until he saw his friends again.

Keth had set more plans in motion, and soon, Earth's media would broadcast a carefully crafted version of events that would maximize support for Earth's visitors while casting the Humanity First movement as violent extremists with no regard for the lives of anyone, human or otherwise, who might get in their way.

The few hostiles who had surrendered had been petty thugs and criminals who had done it for the pay, not the cause. They'd been handed over to local law enforcement, who had been credited with the rescue of the kidnapped victims.

All in all, it had been a success…except for Lily. She'd been wounded, but Vykor had been too distressed to say more than a few words to anyone about how it happened. He was with Lily now, refusing to leave her for even a moment.

Karos had his suspicions about what that meant, and why Vykor, who had never shown any indication of a dragon spirit, had been able to transform into a dragon. A purple dragon, no less. As far as he was aware, such a thing had never happened among his species. Children with parents of different clans were born to one clan or the other. Once again, Vykor had become something unheard of. Frost and flame, the priests were going to be beside themselves when they learned of it.

Megan's hand touched his arm and he looked up to see Jet and Hanna coming toward them, hand in hand. His friend was walking with a slight limp, and there was a faint bruise, already fading, showing beneath the dark stubble on his jaw.

Megan gave a soft cry of relief and ran to Hanna, wrapping the female in a rib-crushing hug. Her words came out with a soft lisp, caused by yet another change in her physical form. She had fangs now. "I'm thorry. I should have been more vigilant. I should haff done more to protect you. You're really alright, aren't you?"

The dark-haired female laughed and hugged Megan back. "I'm okay. Still trying to get my mind wrapped around everything that's happened. After they took us, they wouldn't tell me what happened to you. I thought you were dead!"

"They left me behind as a kind of living ransom note. I'm fine. I'm thorry I failed you."

"You didn't fail me. You came back for us. As a dragon! How did that happen?" Hanna asked, her eyes widening as she looked from Megan to Karos, then smiled a little. "Or can I guess?"

Karos noted that Hanna's eyes were a brilliant shade of gold, and looked over at Jet. His eyes had changed, too. It would appear the Gods had been very busy since last they'd seen each other.

Jet came over and clapped him on the shoulder. "I am very glad to see you again, my friend."

"Not as glad as I am to see you. I should have seen the threat to you and the others. It was my job to protect you, and I failed."

Jet rolled his eyes. "Hanna and I had a bet going to see

which one of you apologized first. Neither of you failed. We were betrayed, but we survived." He looked over at Megan and Hanna, his expression softening. "And while I was gone, you found your mate. Congratulations."

"To you, as well. The Gods had plans for us." Karos looked over to the medical vehicle where Vykor and Lily were. "I hope the Gods are as good to Vykor and the young human female." He lowered his voice and uttered the question he'd been waiting to ask, "Is she the one who betrayed you all?"

Jet shook his head. "She was used by someone she trusted. Believe me, she wasn't part of it."

"How can you be sure?"

Jet grimaced. "Hanna and I were valuable as hostages. They…were not. They were not well treated. We were kept in another part of the building, but we heard…" he trailed off, his face going pale.

"Who shot her?" he asked.

"Her own family. Can you imagine? My family are far from perfect, but from what I saw, Lily's childhood must have been a nightmare."

He'd seen families torn apart by hatred before. It was never easy to watch and he wouldn't wish it on anyone, but what Jet witnessed made it easier to believe that Lily was truly a victim and not a co-conspirator. Karos wanted to believe that, because if that wasn't true, then the Gods had set up Vykor for even more suffering. He couldn't believe that. "Vykor found his mate. I have to believe the Gods would not give him such a gift without having plans for them both. He's something new and powerful."

"Yeah. I noticed. A dragon of both fire and ice." Jet

shook his head. "Every time we come to this planet, something happens that changes one of our worlds."

"And yet, we keep coming back."

There was a joyful cry from the ambulance area, followed by a series of happy barks.

"Who brought a dog?" Megan asked, perplexed.

"She's with Lily. It's a long story," Hanna replied.

Vykor appeared shortly thereafter, garbed in a simple, dark blue outfit of loose-fitting pants and a flowing shirt. He'd conjured the clothing himself, and he'd been smart enough not to try for something too elaborate. He was carrying a female with a riot of blonde curls and a shy smile. She was dressed in a similar fashion to Vykor, though her outfit was a vibrant shade of violet. Following behind them was the largest canine Karos had ever seen, its cavernous jaws open in what appeared to be a canine grin.

"Lily!" Megan and Hanna called out at the same time.

Lily waved and beamed. "I'm okay! It was merely a flesh wound!"

He didn't get the joke, but both Hanna and Megan burst into relieved laughter and rushed to meet her, both of them talking over the other, their every word filled with joy. Lily was important to both of them, and it was clear by the way Vykor cradled her in his arms, she was important to the young dragon, too.

"What happened?" Megan demanded. "Who hurt you?"

He stilled, listening carefully for the answer.

Lily's smile vanished, replaced by shame and a flood of tears. "It was John. He did this. I'm so sorry, Hanna. I didn't know. I swear, I didn't know anything about this. I didn't even know he was part of this stupid group until he walked into my cell."

"I know. John used you. You didn't mean to tell him anything, did you? You always told me he was trouble, and that you didn't want anything to do with him." Hanna said.

"I didn't tell him a thing!" Lily's voice rose. "I told my mom about your necklace because I thought it was a cool gizmo. I never told her I had one, too. I didn't want her to worry about why I might need such a thing. I never thought she'd tell anyone. This is all my fault. I'm so sorry."

"You weren't the one who gassed us, or told your asshole brother we were coming. Kyle did that." Megan took Lily's hand and gripped it tight. "But you did find a way to get your tracker outside the walls so we could find you. How'd you do that, anyway?"

Lily smiled through her tears as she filled the others in on what she'd done. He watched the reunion for a moment longer, then closed his eyes and offered up a silent prayer of thanks to the Lady of Flame and the Lord of Frost for their mercy. Lily would be alright, and Vykor's mate hadn't betrayed anyone. The nightmare was over.

Jet stirred beside him. "I don't know about you, but I'm still in the thrall of the Scorching. Hanna and I need to get back to the embassy, soon."

"It is the same for me. Megan and I will be departing soon." He glanced over at Jet. "How did you manage to claim Hanna while the two of you were under guard?"

The Pyrosian blushed to the roots of his dark hair, though his grin nearly reached from ear to ear. "Humans have a saying. Necessity is the mother of invention."

Karos chuckled. "And the Scorching has no care for such minor problems as locks, guards, or danger."

"Exactly." Jet tilted his head toward Megan. "You were rather inventive yourself, I see."

"That…was an accident. One I imagine I will be apologizing for, for many years."

"A happy accident. The sight of two dragons in the sky was what tipped our captives into a panic. They were prepared for one dragon, but not two."

Karos snorted. "There is nothing these humans could have done to prepare for a Romaki dragon on the attack. With three of us making an appearance? Their fates were sealed."

"Come on, mighty Romaki. It's time we joined the others."

Karos nodded. "And then go our separate ways. I imagine Vykor will take his new mate into the mountains as well."

"Meet you back at the embassy in a few days, then?" Jet said.

"Keth and Eva will be able to update you on all that happened while you were gone." Karos walked over to Megan, wrapping an arm around her waist and tugging her back against his body without speaking. He needed to be near her, but he didn't want to rush the last few minutes she would have with her friends for a few days. They were important to her. Which meant they were destined to become important to him, too.

As he stood there, that truth finally sunk in. He'd come to Earth to escape the past, but he'd never imagined he'd find his future here. A mate. Friends. A job he loved and a chance to make a difference. It was a dream made manifest. Now, all he had to do was make sure that it was all Megan wanted, too. After all, they weren't just mates. They were partners.

MEGAN WAS TORN between her desire to stay with her newly-freed friends and the all-consuming fires of the *rux*. She'd managed to push those needs aside for the rescue, but even as they had waited for word about Lily, the urges had returned threefold. Her skin was hypersensitive, her body aching with needs and wants she couldn't ignore any longer. When Karos drew her back against him, she felt the hard line of his cock pressed into her back, and it was all she could do to resist the urge to rub herself over him like an affection-starved cat.

"*Want mate. Now,*" her dragon complained.

"*Soon,*" she promised the creature.

Hanna was leaning into Jet, too, her fingers idly stroking the back of his arm where it crossed over her waist. Lily was still nestled in Vykor's arms, her eyes as bright as stars as she looked up at the Romaki male with obvious affection and something far more primal and possessive. It was time for them to go. All of them. Six beings had become three couples, and all of them needed time alone with their new mates.

"We should—" Hanna blushed.

"I need to go with Vykor," Lily almost whispered the words.

"Karos and I should go, too."

"But we're coming back. Right?" Lily asked worriedly.

"Of course," Hanna said at almost the same time as Megan.

"Three days from now, we'll all meet at the embassy," Jet stated, and both Romaki nodded in agreement.

"Don't forget to bring comms," Karos said. "Report in when you can, so we know everyone is safe."

Vykor groaned. "Not sure I'm going to be able to think that clearly, but I'll try."

"Do it, or I'll fly over to your bower and tie your tail in a knot," Karos rumbled.

Vykor raised his gaze to the elder dragon, eyes flashing. "You could try." Then he took a deep breath and shook his head. "Sorry. It's hard to think straight right now."

Karos laughed and nodded. "I know."

"When we get back, will you teach Lily and me how what we need to know? I never learned. This… it wasn't supposed to happen," Vykor asked.

"We'll talk as we fly. By the time we part company, you'll know enough to get by. The rest I can teach you when we've all returned." Karos tightened his arm around her waist. "All the new dragons will need instruction."

"Damn skippy. No more crash landings for me," Megan agreed.

Lily's eyes widened and her fair cheeks turned a little green. "We're flying?"

"Don't worry. I'm pretty sure dragons don't get airsick," Megan said with a laugh.

After that, there were hugs, goodbyes, and a few minutes of organization, then it was time to go. She looked up at Karos. "Thank you for keeping your promise."

"Always." He took her hand and lifted it to his mouth

to kiss her fingers. "Come, *sadina*. It's time we set duty aside."

A jolt of lust slammed through her and she nodded eagerly. She was more than ready to leave duty behind and indulge in several days of *rux*-induced debauchery instead.

———

THEY FLEW into the mountains outside the city, Vykor carrying Lily on his back. She was dressed for the weather, now, swaddled in layers of blankets and thick woollen pants as she pointed out various landmarks along their flight path.

As they flew, Karos instructed them on various things, and there were some silences where she assumed he and Vykor spoke privately. She was getting better at flying now, and she was determined to manage a better landing this time around.

The wind was cold, the skies burdened with dark clouds heavy with rain, but the weather didn't bother her at all. She soared over the mist-shrouded peaks, watching the dark green forest flow beneath them like a living carpet. Eventually, they left the others, who flew off toward a meadow that Vykor claimed he'd heard about from the only other Romaki to visit this part of the world – Prince Radek.

Karos flew to a narrow slash of open ground between two thick stretches of forest. The ground was covered in a heavy blanket of untouched snow. It was silent, idyllic, and according to him, it was where they would spend the next few days.

"Where will we stay? There's nothing out here but trees, rocks, and snow."

"Have patience. I will see to your comfort once we have landed."

"With what? I'm a city girl, Big Red. I can rough it when I have to, but I prefer big, fluffy pillows and warm, soft beds to sleeping on rocks or a pine bough bower."

"Have faith in me, sadina. Now, watch me land and then try to do the same."

She did as he said, keeping an eye on his form as he approached the clearing and touched down with an impressive amount of grace for something so large. She did her best to duplicate his moves, and while she still hit the ground hard enough to make the snow jump all around her, she didn't lose her balance or face plant, so she called it a success.

"Transform. I will see to your clothing this time."

She did so, and this time it was a little easier, the change coming faster and with less disorientation. Karos had conjured a thick cloak of black fur for her, resting atop a loose-fitting robe of some soft, thick fabric she didn't recognize. It was a deep crimson and a perfect match for the fur-lined boots that appeared on her feet. She felt like she was wrapped in decadence and warmth, and while her breath frosted in the air, she was as warm as if she'd been standing in her room back at the embassy. She also noticed that all her weapons were set neatly on a small rug by her feet.

He changed forms a few seconds later, appearing in a similar outfit, though his cloak was trimmed in dark red and had a stylized dragon emblazoned across the back.

She was tempted to ask what happened next, but

before she could say anything, Karos raised his hands and began speaking in what she assumed was Romaki. When they got back to the embassy, she really needed to ask about the cognitive augmentation that would allow her to speak his language. Eva had recommended it to her, along with other augmentation packages that would teach her everything she needed to know about Romaki culture and history.

All thoughts about augmentation and learning came to a screeching halt as Karos raised his voice and gestured at the outcropping of rock that filled the far end of the clearing. The snow hissed and melted away, baring the rocks beneath. Within seconds the rock started to glow a brilliant red; the heat it gave off making the air shimmer and dance. She was far enough away she couldn't feel more than a warm breeze on her face, but the rock was hot enough it melted into a thick liquid that flowed across the freshly cleared land like lava.

No, not *like* lava. It *was* lava. And as she watched, the lava began to form itself into a recognizable shape. A house. Walls rose first, rising more than three meters into the air. Windows appeared, along with doorways and finally, a sloping roof. There was too much going on for her to see all of it, but she got the impression that the entire structure was becoming more ornate, with details appearing everywhere. Dragon motifs in blazing reds and yellows, and a thin, translucent material flowed down over the holes she thought of as windows, sealing them against the elements. Steps appeared at the doorway, and then the lava flowed in a gently winding path that stopped just a few feet away from where she stood.

She was still trying to take it all in when Karos spoke,

and she belated realized he'd stopped chanting. "Will it do?" he asked.

"You made us a house of molten stone. And it even has windows! I have no idea how you managed it, but yes, it will more than do. It's amazing, and so are you."

She took a step toward him, but he raised a hand to stop her. "I'm not done, yet. This is an important moment for my species. This bower is my gift to you. It is a demonstration of my abilities and a gesture of my affection. It will have every luxury you can imagine, and while we reside here, It will be a place of pleasure and relaxation where we can get to know each other."

"So, this is our honeymoon?"

He paused for a moment and then smiled. "Yes. At least, that's the closest word you have in your language."

"And one day, I'll be able to do this, too?" She waved to the rock house, which was still throwing off enough heat to rival a small star.

"You will, though not for some time. I have had several centuries to master my magic." He turned back to the house and started speaking in rhythmic phrases, his hands busy drawing designs in the air in front of him.

The stone's surface changed, solidifying as it began to cool. Its surface looked like polished black mirrors, shot through with gleaming veins of crimson and gold that seemed to ebb and flow like miniature rivers. Less than five minutes later, Karos lowered his hands and ceased chanting.

"Is it ready?" she asked him.

"It is." He held out his hand to her and she joined him, almost breathless with anticipation. She wanted to see what he had created, but even more than that, she wanted him.

"*Ours*," her dragon murmured. The thought was accompanied by a powerful surge of lust.

"Yes, he is," she replied out loud.

Karos glanced down at her. "Your dragon?"

"Is very pleased we're finally alone."

"As is mine." He took her hand and raised it to his lips, kissing her fingertips before turning and lifting her into his arms. He carried her up the walkway and into the house. When the door closed behind them, it was as if the entire world vanished, leaving them alone with their desires.

CHAPTER TEN

HE DIDN'T GIVE her a chance to look around before he had her pinned against the newly shut door, his mouth on hers, hungry and demanding. She wrapped her arms around his neck, returning his kiss with one of her own, her voice rising in a needy whimper as lust exploded in her veins.

He held her against the wall with his body, raised one hand, and banished their clothes with a snap of his fingers. His skin was fever-hot, warmer even than the magically heated stone at her back. Tongues twined, mouths mated, and they ground against each other in a frenzy of need that threatened to set the air around them on fire.

When he raised his head again, Karos' eyes nearly glowed with desire, his entire body hard and ready. "I am not good with words, *sadina*, but I want you to know what it means that you are here with me. You are everything I could hope for in a mate. Brave. Strong. Loyal. Loving." He paused to kiss her gently. "Passionate. I do not deserve you. I know that. But I will do all I can to be a good mate to you, now and for the rest of our lives."

She cupped his cheek with her hand, blinking fast to rid herself of the tears his words had caused. She'd given up finding someone who accepted her for who she was, and what she wanted to do with her life. She still didn't know how they were going to make things work, but she knew they'd find a way. They'd have to, because she couldn't imagine trying to live without him. "You are the sexiest, kindest male I know, of any species. I don't know why we were chosen for each other, but I'm going to trust in your gods and mine that this is meant to be. You're mine, and I am yours. Now and forever."

He nodded and lifted her higher in his arms before stepping away from the wall and turning around to show her the inside of the home he'd created for her. "I am yours. And so is everything here."

"I still can't believe you created all this out of nothing." The entire place wasn't much larger than a typical hotel suite, though it was furnished in the most luxurious style imaginable. One area was clearly a dining room, with a polished stone table laden with foods, some of which she recognized and some she'd never seen before. The scent of roasting meat and savoury spices filled the air, along with the sweeter notes of fresh fruit and desserts. The table had benches on two sides, the hard stone covered by a myriad of cushions. The walls still gave off a faint reddish light where the veins of red flowed through the black rock, but most of the light came from a fireplace in the center of the room, where flames flickered over what looked like stone logs.

He stood a little straighter, and a pleased smile touched

his lips. "Anything my mate wishes, I can conjure. Tell me what you desire, *sadina*, and I will make it happen."

"I can't think of anything you didn't already conjure." She waved a hand to a side wall, where the stone had been formed into a deep bathing pool full of steaming water. Flower petals floated on the surface, and more of the petals formed a pathway from where they stood to the foot of a massive bed that took up most of the back wall.

His smile widened. "Good."

"But I can think of one thing I desire and don't have." She pointed to the bed and tried not to blush. "You and me on that bed. Naked and doing all sorts of wicked things to each other."

He growled low in his throat and sprinted to the bed, making her laugh. She was still laughing as they landed on the bed in a tangle of limbs, kissing and touching each other everywhere they could reach.

He came down beside her, draping one long leg over hers as he leaned over her and kissed her until she was shaking with need.

She let her hands run up and down his body, exploring every hard inch of him. Her fingers traced over his scars and he stiffened slightly, reminding her that he wasn't done healing. His body was fine, but his heart and soul still bore the wounds he'd gotten the day he'd lost Tali and the others. Loving her couldn't make that hurt vanish.

Love. Her heart slammed hard against her ribs as the word rolled through her mind. She was going to love him someday, and he would love her. It wasn't a question, it was the truth, and she knew it was surely as she knew her own name.

"What is it?" he asked, raising his head to look down at her with concern.

"What?"

"You're crying?"

"I'm not," the denial was automatic, but she realized her cheeks were wet with tears. "Hey, you just used a contraction!"

He kissed away her tears before answering. "You have affected me in every way imaginable, even the way I speak. But I still want to know why you are crying."

"Because I'm happy. Happier than I think I've ever been."

"So am I." His next kiss slanted across her lips with searing intensity. Passionate and eager, he branded her mouth with his. His low groans of need rolled through her like the sound of distant thunder as he moved over her, covering her with his body and pressing her down into the soft blankets. She parted her legs and he settled between them, never slowing his kisses as they moved.

She buried her fingers in his hair and pulled him closer, arching herself against him in silent invitation.

"Mine," he whispered the word like a strangely possessive prayer.

"Always," she whispered back, and she put her heart and soul into the word.

He uttered another low, shuddering groan and kissed his way down her body, leaving a trail of fire everywhere his lips grazed her skin. He moved slowly, tasting every part of her until his mouth closed on one nipple, making her moan.

It was incredible, but it wasn't enough. She wanted to burn hotter than the sun, to let the heat between them grow to an inferno that consumed them both. "Need you, now."

"I know," he whispered, his fingers stroking the inside of her thigh. "We will do slow another time, then."

"No more slow," she agreed.

He parted her folds with his thumbs and she felt the gentle scratch of his beard against tender flesh. Then, he moved in close, using his tongue flick over the delicate pearl of nerves hidden beneath its hood. Pleasure coursed through her, filling her veins and flooding her senses and she raised her hips to grind herself against his mouth.

She was close to coming within minutes, with Karos' fingers and tongue working her body with such focus that she could barely breathe. When her orgasm came, it hit with the force of a meteor strike, sending her senses flying as she rode uncountable waves of pleasure.

He moved again, his mouth claiming hers as he positioned himself between her legs and claimed her with a slow, steady thrust. After that first move, he stilled, though, and then lifted his head to smile down at her.

"You are perfection, Megan Richards."

"So are you, Karos Zattar, my *sodono*."

His eyes lit up at the word, and then he was moving again, making love to her with hard, ardent thrusts that drove every thought from her head. She lost herself in the pleasure of it, body arched, flesh to flesh, the taste and scent and feel of him infusing her very soul.

As they both neared climax, her dragon stirred in the back of her mind. *"Bind us together. Take. Claim."*

She broke their kiss and tilted her head to one side, then raised her mouth to the side of his throat and bit him, her fangs sinking into his neck with surprising ease. Once again there was a sense of connection, and as Karos bit her in return she exploded into an earth-shattering orgasm. Within the pleasure was something new, a presence. Karos. She could feel him, their energies combining, binding together in new and wonderful ways. When it was over, she was left breathless and dazed, but there wasn't any doubt anymore. There couldn't be, because she finally understood the strength of their bond. They were soulmates, and no matter what the future brought, they would face it together. Partners, lovers, and more. Always.

"*Ours*," her dragon murmured in contentment as Karos withdrew from her and settled at her side before drawing her back into his arms.

"Mine," he declared.

Megan laughed. "My mate and my dragon are both incredibly possessive."

"As it should be. Is there anything else my mate needs from her *sodono*?"

She thought about it for a second, then snuggled into the warmth of his embrace. "I have everything I need, right here."

Karos rumbled in contentment. "That is also as it should be."

She closed her eyes and let herself drift, knowing that soon she'd be asleep. Now that her friends were safe and Karos was with her, she could rest. Everything else, she'd deal with later. Much later.

EPILOGUE

Keth kept them updated on everything that was happening back at the embassy while they were in the thrall of the *rux*, which Karos appreciated. His updates came every few hours, though, which was not appreciated at all, and Karos suspected the damned Pyrosian was doing it on purpose.

Megan didn't think much of those interruptions, either, which was why their comms had been reduced to molten slag by the end of the second day. She'd taken it from him mid-conversation, told Keth to go away, pitched it into the middle of the clearing, transformed, and toasted it to ash before he could react. At least, that was the story he'd tell Keth when they got back.

They'd been in contact with the other couples too, though far less regularly than Keth's updates had been. They'd made preliminary plans that suited everyone and would allow his *sadina* to continue her work. There would be concessions to make in the future, but for now, everything was arranged.

The humans had reacted to the attack and kidnapping with outrage and anger. Even the most uncommitted governments declared the Humanity First movement to be a terrorist organization. All known members were arrested, and their sources of support and finances were cut off. There was still work to be done, but the humans would do most of it. This was their planet, and these were their citizens. Karos and the others would continue to do what they had been doing: reducing the fear through education and outreach while staying watchful and aware.

When he returned, he and Megan would be working together to ensure Kyle was the only member of the movement to infiltrate their embassy. Keth had started the investigation, but after today, they'd return to Vancouver to oversee things . It was the first time in his life that the thought of returning to duty held little appeal. He'd rather spend more time alone with his mate.

Once she'd bitten him, completing their bonding, everything had fallen into place. He still couldn't believe he'd tried to deny she was his mate. She was made for him, just as he had been made for her. One day, he would bring her back to Romak to meet the rest of his family, but that wouldn't happen soon. First, they needed to escort Hanna and Jet to Pyros, and then they would start the work of expanding the Haven Network to include transporting willing females and their offspring to Pyros to start a new life somewhere they would be safe. It was a good mission, one that would fulfill him and his mate for years to come.

Megan rose from the heated pool he'd made for her and walked, still naked and wet, across the stone floor to his side. "You're thinking too much."

The *rux* might be fading, but seeing her naked was all he needed to rekindle the lust of the last few days and set his thoughts aside again.

"Not now that I've seen you. We are not due back at the embassy for a few hours, yet." He swept his mate into his arms and carried her back to bed. The joy and laughter that filled the air came from both of them, and it filled not only the room but the empty parts of his heart. He'd come to Earth looking for a mission. Megan had given him a life. One full of love, laughter, and a chance to help others find lives of their own.

The End

ABOUT THE INTERGALACTIC DATING AGENCY SERIES

Ready for more out of this world romances? The adventure isn't over yet! Fly over to our dating agency website to check out more stories from this multi-author series. The Intergalactic Dating Agency is ready and waiting to set you up with a host of alien hotties from all over the galaxy.

Make a date with your alien match today.

http://romancingthealien.com

Want to read more stories with book boyfriends
that are out of this world?

**Check out Susan Hayes' other Science Fiction Romance
Titles**

The Drift
Double Down
All In
Wild Card
Three of a Kind
No Limit
Blind Bet
Aces Over Queen

Nova Force
Operation Phoenix
Operation Cobalt
Operation Fury

3013: The Series
3013: RENEGADE
3013: STOWAWAY
3013: TARGETED
3013: FATED
3013: SCARRED